Dark Ear

no

The Spore Queen

Debra Castaneda

SHADOW
CANYON
— *press* —

ISBN: 979-8-9877469-8-1
Edited by: Lyndsey Smith, Horrorsmith Editing
Cover design by: James, GoOnWrite.com

To Carolyn

Chapter 1

March 2007

A cold, biting wind swept across the ravaged forest. David Eager stood at the edge of his land, surveying the chaos wrought by the merciless storm. He couldn't help but marvel at his property having been spared.

Surrounded by the ruins of Nils Forest, the Mendocino Wellness Haven cabins remained undisturbed. The vast expanse of trees had served as a barrier against the violent gusts coming down from the mountain, reducing the edges of the old woodland to a tangled mess of shattered trunks and branches.

A freak storm—that's what the forest ranger had called it on the news.

It struck at 7:30 a.m., when he'd been alone in his house. The last guest had checked out the day before, and the next group wasn't due until the weekend. David had cowered in bed for minutes, listening to the howling wind, convinced he'd been imagining the ruckus.

He'd been imagining lots of things lately.

Something hard had slammed against the outside wall of the bedroom, jolting him into action. He'd mustered up the courage to look out the window. Through the early morning light, debris and foliage hurtled past, like a scene out of *The Wizard of Oz.*

It had taken a whole day for the laborers to clean up.

From the wide porch of his stone house, he watched his men going about their work, shaking their heads in disbelief at the untouched grape vines.

David made no effort to help. In the past, he would have joined in, trying to prove he was just a regular guy. But he *wasn't* a regular guy anymore. His once confident strides had shortened to a series of clumsy, unsteady steps. Despite all the tests, doctors were unable to diagnose his growing list of symptoms. But what concerned him the most was what was happening to his mind.

Anxiety twisted in his stomach like a snake. The destruction in the forest was almost a metaphor for his body. The ranger had said the forest would heal itself with time. It had recovered from worse—wildfires, diseases, invasive species, and pests. But he was no forest. His body was damaged beyond repair.

David tensed at the sound of approaching footsteps. The Haven's manager wasn't due for another hour. David didn't turn around. Didn't want to find out he was imagining things again.

"Mr. Eager?" The voice belonged to a young woman. Hesitant. Tentative.

He turned slowly and coughed in surprise.

She was unconventional but stunning. A cascade of golden hair stood out against her smooth brown skin. Her dark eyes were captivating, and her prominent nose gave her a strong, distinctive look.

The wind seemed to grow louder behind him, almost overpowering his voice when he introduced himself. "I'm David Eager."

The stranger couldn't be a guest. The retreat, known for providing a peaceful escape for overworked tech executives, catered to an older crowd.

She smiled, revealing a set of perfect white teeth. "I'm Maria Hart. Radio reporter from San Francisco. I was hoping—"

"That's a long way to come for nothing," he interrupted. "I don't give interviews. If you'd done your homework, you would have saved yourself the drive." His hands twitched with irritation, or maybe something more sinister.

"I know. That's what I tried to tell my boss, but he insisted on sending me anyway." She sighed. "I'm sorry about this. I'm new at the station, and I'm still trying to prove myself. If you would just give me a few minutes of your time, I'd really appreciate it."

Her frankness caught him off guard. The wind whipped Maria's hair across her face, and he noticed a mole above her upper lip. In the past, her youth and beauty might have tempted him. But now, those feelings had gone—another sign of his pathetic decline. Not that David had a chance. She didn't even look thirty, and he was pushing sixty.

Her dark eyes were pleading. "Please. Just five minutes, and I'll be out of here."

David couldn't think of an excuse. Time was no longer of the essence. He had five minutes. Hell, he had the rest of the day. He could stick to his principles and say, "I never talk to reporters." Which was true. Ever since his early days as an entrepreneur seeking investors for his startup, he had avoided speaking to the media.

Until now.

Maria Hart had cornered him, and he found himself giving in to her charming persistence.

"What did you want to talk about?"

Her lips relaxed into a smile. "Nothing controversial. I'm just curious about what led you to sell your company and why you decided to open this place. Can we go inside?"

David's gaze lowered, focusing on the ground. How could he make it to the house without Maria noticing his awkward gait? He would have to concentrate. Take careful steps. With luck, she'd be too busy congratulating herself on her exclusive story to notice the peculiar way he walked.

He needn't have worried. Maria left to retrieve her audio equipment from the car, which gave him enough time to reach the porch unnoticed. When she asked to use the bathroom, he pointed her toward the end of the hallway, hoping she wouldn't wander into his personal space. He didn't like the idea of her seeing his unmade bed with its rumpled sheets.

Outside, the trees swayed in the wind. Inside, Maria was talking. At first, he assumed she was on the phone, but soon after, the young reporter appeared, accompanied by his housekeeper. Anita was doing her best to hide her surprise at the presence of an unexpected guest.

"You want some coffee, Mr. David?" she asked.

"Yes, please, Anita. And some lunch would be nice. Maria's come all the way from San Francisco, so I'm guessing she might be hungry."

Maria perched on the chair next to him, a microphone cable draped across her lap. She flashed a smile at Anita. "That would be amazing, thank you. I'm starving, actually."

As promised, Maria only asked about his retirement—he was tired of working, plain and simple—and the retreat for overworked Silicon Valley executives—no one else had thought of opening one in Mendocino, close enough to drive but far enough to feel like a true getaway.

At his request, Anita served lunch on the porch. Maria ate her meal while wrapped in a green woolen blanket. Her gaze kept drifting to Nils Forest across the sun-drenched meadow. A massive pile of shattered branches and debris sat at the edge of the wide field, ready for the next truck to come and dispose of it all.

"Did you see the windstorm? The coverage looked unreal, like something out of an apocalypse movie."

David nodded. "That's the perfect description."

Maria sipped her coffee and frowned. "The station wants me to do a twofer."

"Oh?" David set down his mug.

"They also want me to cover the storm for a separate story. One of the scientists we talked to says these types of storms are going to become more common and more intense."

David sat back in his chair, stung. He'd flattered himself, fooled into thinking the radio station had sent the reporter all the way up here just for him, but he was merely an afterthought, a way for them to make the most of their trip. Grab a quick interview with the has-been recluse and get more bang for their gas money.

His time with Maria seemed to fly by. She was a rare listener, asking insightful questions. David found himself talking about the stress and exhaustion he'd faced, even telling her about a seizure he'd had ten years into his role as CEO.

"That's terrible," she murmured. Her sad eyes never left his face.

He shook his head. Picked a crumb off his flannel shirt. "I made myself sound so pathetic just now, didn't I?"

Maria plucked off her headphones. "No. You were just being honest. Your old job sounds terrible." She wrinkled her nose. "Some days, the stories I cover are so heartbreaking that I literally go home and cry. My roommate thinks I'm an idiot for becoming a reporter. She says I'm too sensitive. It's like someone who's afraid of blood choosing to be a surgeon."

"Sounds like you're an empath," David commented. He knew a thing or two about personality types—empaths were rare in Silicon Valley.

"That's what my therapist says."

David smiled. "I never thought I'd say this about meeting a journalist, but I've enjoyed our conversation."

David glanced at his phone and was surprised to see it was almost one o'clock. They had been chatting for almost two hours. Maria had one more story to cover, which included a ten-mile trip to the ranger station and who knew what else. It would be a draining day, followed by a long drive back to San Francisco on winding roads.

"Do you have a place to stay for the night?" he asked.

A look of annoyance crossed her face. "There's no budget for travel. I'll have to suck it up and cover a motel myself."

"What if you stayed here? In one of the cabins? They're vacant anyway. Anita can make you some dinner and leave it in the fridge for when you get back."

Maria sat up a little straighter, and she smiled. "Seriously? That would be amazing. Thank you so much! And that would give me time to explore the forest. I had no clue your place was right next to it, so it's super convenient." She pointed toward the trailhead. "Would you like to come with me and show me around? You must know it really well, and I'd love to get your perspective on the storm damage."

The thought of trying to keep up with this young, energetic woman filled him with trepidation. Just maneuvering around the flat paths on his property was already enough of a challenge.

"I really wish I could," he replied, his voice carrying a hint of regret, "but I have some things to take care of here, unfortunately."

Later, David watched Maria emerge from Cabin No. 6, dressed for hiking in a robin's-egg-blue jacket and boots, her hair pulled back in a ponytail. When she spotted him through the window, she waved, and he returned the gesture. She disappeared into the forest, her audio equipment bag slung over her shoulder.

After hours had passed and the sun began to slide behind the trees, Maria appeared at the door, panting as if she'd just finished a run. "You won't believe what I've found out there. It's incredible. The forest is covered in fungus. The ranger said the mycelium comes to help the forest recover."

"Mycelium?" David echoed, intrigued. He knew there were mushrooms in the forest, but he didn't know much about them.

"Yes, mycelium. They're these white roots that sprout from the fungus or something. At least, that's what I think he said. There are mats of them everywhere, and they're so dense they look like blankets. This is so cool because I've been wanting to cover more environmental stories, and this one is fascinating. I was devastated when I saw how many trees were knocked down. At first, I thought the white stuff was a disease, until the ranger explained what mycelium does. And while I was out there, I found some crazy-looking mushrooms, so I picked some to show to the ranger. And guess what they were?"

Her excitement was contagious, and David found himself smiling. "What?"

Maria's dark eyes glittered. "Magic mushrooms! The kind that makes people trip out. Or at least, that's what he thought." Maria glanced down at her phone. "I have to go.

I'm meeting with a mushroom expert. He's going to explain everything to me. I'll see you later. When I'm done."

Maria turned on her heels and sprinted back toward the trailhead, feet pounding against the ground as she ran through the trees.

The forest seemed to swallow her whole.

Chapter 2

October 2007

Of all the words in the English language, "no" was Amy Matthews's least favorite. Especially when it came from her least favorite person at the radio station—the pompous jerk at the assignment desk.

"I hate crime stories," he said dismissively, when she pitched going to Mendocino to cover the disappearance of Karl Ackerman.

Amy didn't give up that easily. "Maybe it isn't a crime. He's the fifth person to disappear in that area, counting Maria. Maybe something else is going on."

"Like what?" Ronald snorted. "Convince me."

"People are posting on a forum I've been following that there's something weird going on at Nils Forest—"

"As in?" Ronald interrupted.

Amy's hands tightened into fists, and she fought to keep her expression professional. Ronald had a punchable face— eyebrows perpetually furrowed, mouth turned down, and stubble reaching just above his prominent Adam's apple. He annoyed the shit out of her.

However, Amy either had to convince him or miss out on the opportunity to pursue the Maria Hart story. She'd never tell Ronald, but Karl Ackerman was simply a means to an end: getting to Mendocino to find Maria Hart.

"As in, strange phenomena. No one else is reporting on it. At least not yet." She paused, letting the implications sink in; Ronald loved beating the commercial stations. "Someone up in Mendocino posted that four members of the search team for Ackerman ended up in the ER after becoming dizzy and disoriented. They kept falling down, and one of them couldn't stop throwing up. Two had to be carried out on stretchers."

Ronald cupped his chin in his hands, eyes widening. "You're kidding? What do they think happened to them?"

"Still waiting for tests to come back."

"What do the police think happened?"

"Who the hell knows because there's no one up there to demand answers from the police chief."

"So, these are just rumors on the interweb tubes?" Ronald scoffed.

By the gleam in his eyes, Amy knew she had him hooked. All she needed now was to reel him in. Patience wasn't her strongest quality.

"Right now, we have the advantage. We've got a jump on the story—"

"But it's just some rando on Reddit, or whatever. You don't know if it's even legit."

Since smacking Ronald wasn't an option, Amy settled on wagging her finger at him. "That's where you're wrong. I called the hospital and confirmed it. And not only that, the nurse I spoke to was super chatty and mentioned this wasn't the first time it's happened. Other people have gotten sick in Nils. He said the ranger's office has been trying to figure it out, but so far, no luck."

Ronald straightened, clasping his hands together on the desk and biting his lip. "What did the ranger's office say?"

Amy held his gaze. "I don't know yet. It's the kind of conversation that should happen in person, don't you think? If I call, they'll just come up with some bullshit excuse to avoid talking to me. Plus, before I meet with anyone official, I need to track down those people who got sick and get them on the record. Get some sound. Five people, Ronald...Five. *Poof.* Gone. Without a trace. It has to be connected to whatever is making these folks sick. That's what people are saying on Reddit, and it makes sense to me too. We gotta jump on this before some other reporter gets onto it."

Ronald sat back in his chair, sighed, then threw up his hands. "Okay, fine. I still have some leftover budget from that documentary that never materialized, but you'll have to do this on the cheap. Why don't you get up there and start working on it? We can figure out the timeline once you've made some progress." He opened his desk drawer and pulled out a company checkbook. "Here's an advance. And be sure to keep all your receipts, unlike the last time."

Amy tucked the check into a pocket. She forced a smile and said, "Thanks, Ronald." Words she thought would never leave her lips.

"We should hang out sometime," he called after her.

Amy managed to make it to the stairwell before she gagged.

Chapter 3

Amy headed for the basement to see the chief engineer about a piece of equipment causing her endless frustration. As the newest reporter on staff, she had been assigned an old cassette recorder, functional but too bulky to easily lug around.

She found Ken in his chaotic office, surrounded by stacks of broadcast equipment and piles of boxes. "Kenneth, can I please, please trade this thing for something from this century?"

Ken spun on his stool to meet her gaze. With his tiny eyes, upturned nose, and white whiskers, he resembled an adorable mole. "That is the most dependable piece of equipment we have, Miss Matthews. Has it ever let you down? Ever?"

She tilted her head back and let out an exasperated sigh. Ken was not a fan of new technology. He'd been dragged, moaning and groaning, into the digital age.

"Never," she admitted. "I actually kind of love it, but it's a bit bulky. I'm going to Mendocino to cover the story about the missing tech guy, and I'll probably have to go into Nils Forest. It would be helpful to have something a little lighter."

She was also annoyed about using a recorder reliant on cassette tapes, but there was no point mentioning it. Ken loved them.

He frowned. "Well, it *is* a tad oversized for that kind of fieldwork. Let me see what else I have." With a martyred sigh, he stood and made his way to the closet. A few moments later, he emerged with a Marantz PMD in hand. Small, lightweight, and digital.

Amy had to resist the urge to snatch it from his grasp. "Can I keep it?"

The crease between Kenneth's eyes deepened. "Only if you promise not to drop it. I was planning on giving it to you once you passed your probation."

"That was months ago," Amy said through clenched teeth. "Can I get a new mic? Mine's kind of janky."

"It's only janky, as you call it, because you don't know how to take care of your stuff," Ken chided, disappearing again into the closet. With a scowl, he placed a long box on the counter. "If Maria had taken the old Marantz like she was supposed to, when she went to Mendocino, we might have more information about what happened to her."

Amy snapped her head up from inspecting her new mic. "What do you mean?"

"Instead of using the equipment I assigned her, Maria decided to buy her own fancy-schmancy digital recorder. She always seemed to have plenty of money. But you know that, right, since you were roommates?"

Amy nodded. That much was true. She and Maria had been roommates in college and then moved together into a place Maria's family had bought her. Maria rarely talked about her adoptive family, but between the flat, her car, and her clothes, Amy knew they had money.

Amy sat down, frowning. "I don't get it. Why do you think we'd have more information if she'd taken the old Marantz instead?"

"It's easy to keep track of cassettes. You write on the label, and you know what you've got. But with that damn thing she bought, it's way too easy to lose tracks. Or files, I guess you call them now. You can delete them or record over them way too easily."

"Didn't the police find her recorder in the woods? They must have listened to what was on it."

"That's right. They brought it here, and we listened too. There wasn't much of significance. Just a couple of files. But for all the time she'd spent up there, there should have been more. But it was too easy to erase things with those units, which is why I refused to order them. They weren't worth the hassle or money."

"What happened to the recorder?"

"The police gave it back to us. Technically, it belonged to Maria and should have been given to her mother, come to think of it. But honestly, it never crossed my mind, and no one else ever mentioned it."

Amy's jaw dropped in disbelief. "Do we still have it?"

"Of course we do," Ken said, voice rising. "Do you think I sold it on eBay or something?"

Amy looked around, as if expecting the recorder to materialize. "Can I listen to it?"

For a moment, Amy was sure Ken would refuse. The engineer was approaching seventy and had been at the station for as long as anyone could remember. He acted like he owned every piece of equipment in the building.

Ken drummed his fingers on the counter, forehead wrinkling. "I don't see why not. It's just sitting there, collecting dust. But do me a favor and keep it between us. I'm just letting you borrow it because you two were friends."

Minutes later, Amy was heading up the stairs, clutching a small cardboard box with her new gear and the ridiculously small recorder once belonging to Maria.

Chapter 4

David stirred awake, rubbing the crust from his eyes. Another rough, nightmare-filled night had followed another visit from the police.

"Parkinson's?" The older officer had watched David shuffle across the living room.

"I wish," David replied brusquely. "It's Lewy body dementia. I wouldn't wish it on my worst enemy."

Hallucinations were a hallmark of the disease, and David's were terrifying. Shadows in the forest sometimes took human form. Awful shrieks came from the walls.

So far, his hallucinations were all sight and sound. They hadn't included his sense of touch, which he had feared since being warned by his doctor. The most common tactile hallucination was the most horrific: the feeling of one's skin being stretched over the head, followed by the sensation of internal organs shifting inside the body.

So far, he'd avoided that nightmare, but he did struggle with bouts of paranoia. David had begun to feel like he wasn't safe in his own home, suspecting Anita had been replaced by an impostor and that his manager was sabotaging the Wellness Haven.

He wasn't ready to admit himself to a care facility and hoped he could avoid it forever. David had plenty of money, after all. So, he hired caretakers to help him when he needed it, and they stayed out of sight so he could pretend they weren't there. David was determined to make the most of his life. Until he couldn't anymore.

"Time to face the day," he muttered, dragging his tired body out of bed.

David stood by the window and stared at the meadow, replaying the police interview in his head. A young man, Karl Ackerman, had been a guest at David's retreat center and disappeared during a walk in the forest—another mystery rooted in the same woods where Maria Hart had gone missing six months ago.

This time, the police hadn't treated him as a suspect. Not like when Maria vanished. Back then, they'd even taken him in for questioning. But not now. Now their pity was almost worse than their previous accusations.

David dressed slowly, feeling the weight of his exhaustion but grateful his limbs were cooperating. He picked up his three-pronged cane and made his way out into the crisp air.

The farm manager, Bill, hurried toward him from across the meadow. Bill had a round face with a warm smile and a ruddy complexion.

"You're looking good today," Bill commented, eyebrows raised in surprise.

David hadn't stepped foot outside for three days straight. "Liar," he replied gruffly.

Bill turned, surveying a fallow plot of land. "We'll have the barley planted before you know it."

He extended his arm toward David, who grudgingly took hold of it—David didn't need another fall.

"The police interviewed me when they were done with you," Bill said as they made their way across the meadow. "And the workers too. I just hope to God one of them isn't a killer. They're good workers and all, but who knows what some of these guys got up to in Mexico. They could have worked for the cartels, for all we know."

David let out a small cough. "You've been watching too many crime shows. And since when did you have a problem with people from Mexico?"

David's hand tightened on Bill's arm in an involuntary spasmodic squeeze.

"I don't have a problem with Mexicans." Bill's voice rose.

"Then don't talk like someone who does." Bill was an excellent farm manager, but David wasn't about to put up with any nonsense.

"Yeah, well. Sorry. I guess all this is just messing with my head. That makes five now, doesn't it? Starting with Maria Hart. I told the police they ought to close down that forest until they can find out what happened to those people, but they said they couldn't do that, on account of it's public land and it's too big to patrol."

David looked down at the uneven ground beneath his feet, memories of Maria flooding his thoughts. What could have happened to her? Kidnapped? Raped? Body buried where no one could find it?

They arrived at the field and paused, taking in the land before them. The unused tiller sat on the edge of the plot. David had suggested trying no-till planting, wanting to be more environmentally friendly, but Bill argued the soil was too compact and overrun with weeds. If they wanted to see a successful harvest sooner rather than later, their only option was to use machinery to bust up the soil.

Bill patted the green tractor that would pull the tiller. "I might just take this baby for a ride myself." He laughed. "Why let the other guys have all the fun?"

David was too busy examining the rotor assembly to respond. There was something unusual coating the tines—a peculiar white growth with a fuzzy texture curling around the sharp steel. It snaked its way up the frame, partially covering the green-painted structure. The same fibrous material could be seen crawling across the massive tires of the tractor.

David pointed. "What's that, Bill?" His voice quavered.

Bill squatted to get a closer look. "I'm not sure," he finally said, rubbing his chin. "Could be mold or mildew. Funny. It wasn't here yesterday when they delivered the tiller, so whatever it is grew fast."

David scanned the back assembly of the tiller. The fibrous strands were wrapped tightly around the metal cover, some tendrils trailing to the ground. A thick hairy mat about six inches wide coiled out toward the nearby forest. It was coming from the woods.

Bill reached down to remove the white threads clinging to the tiller. By the way Bill was tugging, David could see it was no easy task.

"Looks like we're going to have to cut this damn stuff off."

David thought for a moment. "How about wetting it down and scrubbing it off? Might be easier."

Bill's face lit up with a grin, and he snapped his fingers. "There you go. That's what we'll do. We'll give this stuff a good scrub."

He hurried off and returned with a camp chair for David. Bill then pulled a hose from the nearby shed and reached into his pocket for a stiff-bristled brush.

David watched Bill work to remove the mysterious growth from the tiller and the tractor tires. Eventually, David's gaze shifted to the fibrous trail leading into the forest. With some effort, he pushed himself out of the chair and went over to inspect it.

The texture resembled thick, course, wet hair matted together. He cautiously extended his cane, prodding at it.

David's heart skipped a beat when the fibrous mass began to wriggle.

Or did it?

David rubbed his eyes, wondering if his mind was playing tricks on him again. But when he looked back down, the thing was still there, writhing ever so slightly. He stabbed it with the end of his cane, rotating it forcefully and yanking upward. The sudden motion almost made him lose his balance. A tangle of thin strands dangled from the cane.

His fingertips grazed the fibrous threads, and a shiver ran along David's spine. The pieces smelled like the underside of an old log rotting in the damp woods. A bead of sweat trickled down his back. His grip faltered, and the cane slipped from his hand.

"I think it's some kind of fungus," he said.

Bill turned, frowned, then quickly nodded in agreement. "That makes sense. There's all kinds of mushrooms in the forest."

"Probably," David replied. His body suddenly felt weighed down. He turned toward the forest, remembering the last time he had seen Maria Hart.

She had mentioned observing fungus everywhere. What had she called it? His exhausted mind struggled to dredge up the word.

Mycelium. That was it. Mycelium. White fibers that lived beneath the forest floor. That's what they were dealing with now. He was sure of it. If only he knew what it meant.

The next morning, David approached the tiller with a strange sense of dread. Despite Bill's efforts to scrub them away the day before, the white filaments had returned overnight. The tendrils glowed eerily in the early light, seeming to pulse with a strange energy—as if they were alive and aware of his presence.

In the distance, Bill's truck roared up the long gravel drive.

David's gaze remained fixed on the unusual growth. He braced himself against the tractor and cautiously extended his hand to touch the sinewy material. But as soon as his fingertips made contact, the stuff seemed to move under his touch, and he recoiled with a gasp.

Bill appeared at his side and gave a low whistle. "What do you make of that?"

David let out a weary sigh. "I think it doesn't want us to use the tiller."

Bill pulled a utility knife from a pocket, flicked it open, and carefully sliced off a small piece of the white growth before carrying it off toward the shed. "I think it's time we get a sample of whatever the heck this is and send it to someone smarter than us. Well, smarter than me, anyway."

David eyed the white fungal trail disappearing into the forest. The sight sent a prickle of alarm coursing up his spine.

Chapter 5

Beset by restlessness and a desire to be alone, David sent his housekeeper into town to pick up his favorite Thai food.

If he took it slow, he could make it across the meadow and back again before Anita returned. He didn't want to catch another lecture about the risks of venturing outside on his own.

With some difficulty, he put on his coat, grabbed the handles of his walker, and made his way down the ramp. He hated the ramp—another reminder of his deteriorating body.

The sun dipped behind the horizon, its fading light casting shadows along the forest floor, and a dense fog crept in among the trees. The scent of pine and decaying leaves permeated the air.

The chill seeped through his jacket and settled into his bones. But despite the cold and gloom, he found himself drawn to the edge of Nils Forest. He couldn't shake the feeling something was off about it—had been for a long time now, even before those white fungal threads appeared on the tiller. Maybe if he got closer to the woods, he could see far enough into the trees to reassure himself all was as it should be and the vague unease plaguing him was just the product of his diseased imagination. In the distance came the haunting chorus of crows.

David picked his way across the meadow, dry twigs snapping and crunching underfoot. A gust of wind whipped through, and he wished he'd brought a scarf to shield his face from the cold. Using the walker was always a challenge, requiring his complete focus. It was even more complicated outside. The uneven ground forced him to lift and place the walker with each step. He struggled forward, his legs shaking, and David started to sweat from the physical strain.

A sound caught his attention. It was coming from the treetops. Something was moving up there. A flock of birds, maybe.

No. Not birds.

Not small distinct shapes, but a shadow amidst the quivering branches. At first, it was just a dark blur, but as David squinted, it became clearer and began to take on a recognizable shape.

No. His eyes were lying. His mind was playing tricks on him. Again.

A woman glided through the darkness, her movements silent and swift. She pushed aside branches, peering down at him. Her skin was golden brown, her features familiar, long hair trailing behind. David rubbed his eyes, blinking, hoping it was just a trick of the fading light. He blinked again, but she was still there, hovering in the air.

"Maria?" David called out. His voice trembled with a mix of hope and fear.

It couldn't be her. It couldn't be real. And yet, David knew it *was* Maria. He could feel it in his bones.

The figure retreated, positioning herself just behind the closest pine tree. She was suspended in midair, her eyes locked on his as if enticing him to join her.

David was unable to tear his gaze away from the beautiful, haunting apparition. "Is this what happened to you? Did you fly away?"

No reaction from the figure. It couldn't be Maria, with her hair now long and unruly. When had she vanished? Long enough for her hair to grow so much? Long enough to learn how to fly?

People. Do. Not. Fly.

His hands clenched the walker, knuckles turning white, and he tried to will the apparition away.

"What do you want?" he shouted.

Her silence taunted him.

Terror coursed through his veins, not because of the flying woman, but because this could be a sign of his final descent into Lewy body dementia. He wasn't afraid of a woman floating in the air, but of his break with reality.

David had experienced hallucinations before, but they were never this vivid and all-consuming. In the past, he could always grasp a shred of reality, some small part of his brain holding out and signaling that, if he could just wait, he'd snap back. But now, while she hovered in the air, he felt no hope of escaping.

"Leave me alone!" David's voice cracked with terror. "I'm sick. Go away."

The figure slowly turned and vanished into the thickening fog.

David let out a guttural cry. He wanted to run, run back to his house, but his body betrayed him. With his walker, he stumbled through the mist toward the lights and safety. When he reached the ramp, he veered off course and instead lurched toward the cabin where Maria Hart had stayed. It had gone unused since she disappeared. His retreat manager said it was ridiculous not to rent it out, yet for some inexplicable reason, David had insisted on keeping it empty. He'd even had another larger cabin built to replace it.

With a shaking hand, he slid the electronic key card into the slot and used his walker to push open the door. He flipped on the light, and his breath caught as he took in the scene before him.

The cream-colored walls were covered in dark streaks. A mat of hairy white stretched across the floor and snaked up the chairs and legs of the table next to the window. The same stuff that had covered the tiller—Mycelium. That's what the lab tests had confirmed. An ordinary fungus.

The bed had been transformed into an otherworldly landscape.

First the levitating woman, and now this.

A riot of mushrooms in strange shapes and colors sprouted from the bed. Some were delicate and pale; others were robust and earthy. A cluster of golden mushrooms protruded shelf-like from a bedpost. Next to an easy chair, a giant mushroom the deep burgundy color of wine grew as large as a footstool.

The oppressive fungal growth pressed in from all sides, and David's chest tightened. The moist, dense air weighed on him, the pungent odor of wet soil and decay filling his nostrils.

He barked out a cough that turned into a wail. "What's happening?"

It had to be his new meds. He should never have taken his latest dose with that wine. The doctor had warned him. David shuddered and edged toward the door, desperate to escape the fruiting madness within the cabin.

The cluster of dark mushrooms on the bed began to sway gently. David didn't know much about mushrooms, but he recognized these by their pitted texture. Morels. Served as an appetizer by a local restaurant.

A whisper, barely audible, called out his name. It was coming from the bed.

His heart pounded, and he strained to listen.

"David."

There it was again. He hadn't imagined it. The morels were calling his name. He was standing on the precipice of something terrible that could lead to a frightening discovery or a permanent break from reality.

David inched toward the bed, his walker creaking with each step. Something caught the wheels and brought him to a sudden stop. He glanced down and immediately spotted the problem—white strands of mycelium snaking through the axel of the wheels. David gave a mighty push. The wheels broke free of their restraints, the sudden movement nearly toppling him in the process. And then he was standing at the side of the bed.

The morels had formed a ring. Inside it, a shape pressed against the underside of the comforter.

A face began to emerge. A woman's face.

The blood in his veins turned to ice, freezing him in place. David felt like he was on the brink of an unfathomable abyss.

The mouth in the face opened. Whispered his name.

The morels were growing now, taller. Reaching for him. David heard himself scream as he lurched toward the door.

Debra Castaneda

Chapter 6

The wind howled through the trees, branches trembling and groaning. Lori Chambers sat in her car, gripping the steering wheel. She was parked near the entrance of Mendocino Wellness Haven because starting with David Eager seemed easier than beginning with Julian.

It was her first encounter with Nils Forest in decades. She'd avoided the town since she was a teenager. The memories had been too painful. The woods loomed on the other side of the meadow, dark and forbidding—the place where her daughter had later disappeared.

Lori's throat tightened, an unrelenting pressure squeezing from the outside in. It came in waves, moving slowly downward. She took deep belly breaths. When the sensation had finally passed, Lori sighed in relief. Sometimes, the coping techniques she'd learned worked. Sometimes, they didn't. Now was not the time for a panic attack.

Hers was the only vehicle in the lot. The modern cabins had a deserted air about them, but lights blazed in the windows of the main house. A sign pointed guests to the back entrance.

She still hadn't decided what to say to David Eager. He was an eccentric recluse. It was possible he wouldn't even speak to her. And even if he did, what could he possibly tell her he hadn't already told the police?

Lori wondered if he'd ever been a suspect. Or perhaps one of his employees.

A gust of wind shook the car, startling Lori out of her thoughts. She looked around, taking in the desolate beauty of the forest on the other side of the meadow.

Lori's memories of the forest were tainted by loss and darkness, but it hadn't always been so foreboding. That summer, it had been glorious, filled with light and secret hideaways where she and Julian could escape.

Maria had vanished in the same place where she was conceived. It was almost too much for Lori to comprehend. She hoped her conversation with David Eager would be more productive than the short meeting she'd had with the police chief that morning.

Troy Moses had accepted her explanation about being Maria's biological mother without question.

When he asked, gently, why she had taken so long to come see him, she'd let out a despairing moan.

"It sounded like you were on top of it. I cannot comprehend how my daughter has not been found, after all this time. You got her car and tape recorder. What exactly have you been doing?"

Troy Moses had a tall, bony frame, with narrow eyes and pockmarked skin. He bristled. "We've done everything we can think of, ma'am. There was no activity on her credit card and nothing unusual about her phone records. We've combed through the forest many, many times, and aside from her tape recorder, there is no sign of her. It's like she walked into the woods and vanished into thin air. We've interviewed her friends and co-workers and—"

"You never interviewed me," Lori had interrupted, resentment in her voice. The police had talked with her aunt, Erika Hart—Maria's adoptive mother.

Chief Moses frowned. "That's not true, Ms. Chambers. We spoke to you briefly on the phone, but there wasn't much you could tell us. Let's schedule a time to talk in a few days, shall we? Right now, I've got a search for Karl Ackerman underway." He paused and placed a hand on her shoulder. "We're not giving up, Ms. Chambers, but please understand the challenges we're facing. That forest spans nearly a million acres, and it's got some treacherous terrain. We're still hoping to find out what happened to your daughter and the others. We had a powerful storm last week that caused significant erosion. Sometimes that uncovers what's hidden underneath."

He let his words drift off. She'd understood his meaning well enough.

Debra Castaneda

Chapter 7

Lori emerged from the 4Runner and was immediately hit by a blast of chilly air, the wind tugging at her hair. She inhaled, taking in the scent of pine trees and wood smoke. When she glanced over at the stone house, she saw a man standing in one of the windows. His mouth was open wide, and he banged on the window frame with a cane, as if screaming for help.

A woman came dashing around the side of the house.

"Sorry, but we're closed," she called out. "We don't take walk-ins."

Lori's gaze shifted toward the window, but the man with the cane was no longer there. She slammed the door of the truck, a signal she would not easily be deterred from her mission.

"I'm not looking for a place to stay," she said. "I have a house in town. I'm here to see David Eager."

The woman frowned. Around fifty. Sharp, angular features and short black hair in a pixie cut. "Do you have an appointment?"

Lori shook her head. "No, but I was hoping he could spare a moment to see me. My daughter is Maria Hart. She was last seen here before she went missing."

The woman's mouth fell open, a hand coming to rest against her breastbone. "Oh. I see. We get some people driving up, thinking it's a bed and breakfast. I'm sorry…"

Lori wondered whether the woman was sorry her daughter was missing or that she couldn't give her a room.

The woman extended her hand. "I'm Pat. I manage the retreat, and I'm David's assistant."

She quickly looked over her shoulder as if expecting her boss to suddenly appear.

"Unfortunately, he's not up to seeing anyone at the moment. But since you're from the area, why don't you leave your contact information with me, and I'll get back to you if David's willing to meet with you." Her smile remained cool and professional.

Lori shifted her weight from one foot to the other. "I really need to speak with him. It'll only take a few minutes." A pleading note had crept into her voice, unbidden.

Pat let out an audible sigh and turned to look back at the house just as the front door opened and a slight figure stepped out onto the porch.

Lori stared at the man, transfixed. He didn't look anything like she had imagined. She'd only seen him in professionally shot photos. His head was topped with a profusion of dark hair. His eyebrows were thick and jutted over his deep-set eyes. He had a strong nose and a wide mouth. In the photos, these bold features suggested a tall, powerfully built man, but in reality, he stood at average height, with the tight, compact body of a teenager.

"Mr. Eager?" she called.

He nodded. "Are you the inspector?" His voice was slightly nasal and thin.

Pat cleared her throat, taking a step toward Lori. Her voice was low and filled with warning. "I told you, he's not well."

Lori looked past her at David Eager. "You met my daughter, Maria Hart. I wanted to ask you a few questions, if that's all right."

At the mention of Maria's name, the man swayed and gripped the porch railing. "I didn't know her. She came to interview me. The police know all about it." He gestured toward a row of cabins located far from the main stone house. "That's where she was supposed to stay. It's all wrong now."

Pat gave her a look that said, "I told you so," before shrugging as if she had no responsibility for whatever happened next.

Lori took a step toward the house. Whatever ailed David Eager wasn't as mundane as the flu, but he seemed too young to have Alzheimer's. She needed to proceed with caution.

"Are you the inspector?" David repeated. "I told Pat to call them."

Lori took a deep breath. She'd been prepared to be rebuffed. Prepared for grudging, unhelpful answers. David Eager was a rich man and a recluse. If he refused to speak with her, she had no power to compel him. This version of David Eager was unexpected, but it presented an opportunity she was ready to seize.

"I'm Maria Hart's mother," she repeated. "But I work in commercial real estate. Can I help you with anything?"

David's brow creased. "Commercial real estate?" As if the tech titan had never heard the term.

"Inspections are part of a real estate transaction. If you need an inspector, I'd be happy to take a quick look at whatever is concerning you. Offer an outside opinion?"

Pat grimaced. "Oh, please. Do not encourage the man."

David Eager seemed to brighten. "I'd like that. A second opinion is always a good thing, and who knows when that inspector is going to arrive."

Lori watched him cautiously descend the ramp, leaning on a walker for support. He shuffled toward her, his head hung low.

A lump formed in her throat. "Did you have a stroke, Mr. Eager?"

His head lifted. "A stroke? No, that would be preferable. What I'm dealing with is frontal lobe dementia. You caught me on one of my better days, so that's saying something."

Judging by Pat's intense glare, this could be her only opportunity to talk with the frail man. Lori began slowly walking closer. "You said something is wrong with the cabin where Maria stayed?"

A shadow crossed over his face, deepening the dark circles under his eyes. "There was something very wrong with it last night."

She detected a hint of fear in his voice as he continued.

"Pat says it looks fine to her, but I'm afraid it comes at night. It's happened before."

"I understand," Lori lied. She felt like Alice tumbling down the rabbit hole and into a world where nothing was as it seemed.

Eager led the way. The cabins, with their modern designs, were arranged in a semi-circle around an enormous stone fire pit and deep wooden chairs. Lori counted eight cabins and a building seemingly serving as a dining hall and gathering place. Constructed of wood, it had a slanted roof and rows of French doors opening onto a patio of fieldstone pavers. Inside were small tables and lodge-style furniture arranged in cozy groupings. Next to that building was a small stone structure with a discreet sign labeling it as a massage studio.

Lori had researched Mendocino Wellness Haven. Guests were required to complete a questionnaire. There were two conditions: they had to work in high tech, and they had to agree to a strict no-device policy during their stay. Rates were not published. Eager decided who got to visit, and those who did raved about their stays.

"This is it," he said when they finally arrived at Cabin No. 6. He eyed the door warily and searched through his jacket pocket, eventually producing a key card.

David gave her the card and stepped aside. The lines etched on his face looked more pronounced in the dull grayness of the morning. His mouth twitched. In the distance, a door slammed. Pat had disappeared. Lori was alone with David now, but there was no telling how long that would last.

She slid the card into the reader, and a small light flashed green. Her pulse quickened as she pushed open the door to peer inside. David's unease was infectious. The wide shutters were closed, making it difficult to see anything within.

David flapped an impatient hand. "Turn on the light."

Lori fumbled in the darkness until her fingers found the switch, and she let out a relieved sigh. There was nothing unusual or alarming about the room. It was large and airy. Clean, modern lines in pale birch wood, chairs upholstered in a tasteful gray and yellow plaid, with a matching throw folded neatly at the foot of the bed. Three landscapes hung on the walls, painted by a local artist whose name Lori recognized.

David made no attempt to enter the cabin. When Lori glanced over her shoulder, he was still on the porch, biting a fingernail.

"Is there something specific you wanted me to look at, Mr. Eager?" she asked from just inside the threshold, anxious to shift the conversation to Maria.

His face contorted. He seemed to be thinking something over. "Fungus," he finally said.

"Fungus?" she echoed. "Like...mold?"

David shrugged. "Maybe. It was all over the place yesterday, like an infestation. Pat wasn't working, so she didn't see the room until today. But I don't trust her anymore. She's been trying to get me into an assisted living facility, but I know what she's really up to. She wants to steal this place for herself. She can't do it, though. I've got lawyers to protect me. When I told her about the mushrooms, she called my doctor without my permission. I warned her if she tried any more tricks like that, she's out."

Lori studied him for a moment. He seemed remarkably articulate despite his illness. Then again, from everything she'd read about him, he was a remarkable man. A decamillionaire by the time he was forty. Lived a simple lifestyle. No mansions, exotic cars, or art collections. No partner. No kids.

She stepped inside the room, sniffed, and detected a faint musty odor.

The buildings were relatively new, but it wasn't unusual to find some mold in damp wooded areas like this one. Lori checked the walls, ceilings, and walk-in closet before moving onto the bathroom. As expected, no expenses had been spared there either. Minimalist luxury at its finest. If the cabin hadn't been aired out in a while, that could account for the smell.

"I don't see any mold," she announced. "Would it be all right if we talked about my daughter now? I promise not to take up too much of your time."

"Not in there," he said. There was a slight tremble to his voice.

Lori wondered what he'd seen that had left him so frightened.

Chapter 8

Lori followed David Eager to the main house. Once inside, she took in her surroundings.

It was deceptively spacious, with a grand stone fireplace dominating the living room. A fire crackled behind a brass grate. Wide plank floors added to the rustic charm of the house, and the open floor plan revealed a beautiful farmhouse-style kitchen with white wooden cabinets. Lori's gaze wandered toward the back of the house. A gate stretched across the bottom of the stairs leading to a second floor, possibly meant as a reminder to Eager to stay off them.

The overall effect was simple and inviting.

A tiny woman appeared in the kitchen and startled, bustling around the counter. "I'll make coffee for you and your guest, Mr. David," she announced.

Lori smiled and gave a grateful wave. She was desperate for some caffeine.

David eased himself into a chair. "Maria didn't resemble you much," he said without preamble. "I would never have guessed that the two of you were related."

Lori's stomach sank at his use of the past tense.

"No. She takes after her father."

David tilted his head and studied her. "You're nice-looking, but she was beautiful."

Lori let out a bitter laugh. "You really know how to hand out the compliments, Mr. Eager."

From the kitchen, Anita clapped her hands. "That's not very nice, Mr. David."

David grimaced. "That's Anita's way of telling me to watch my mouth. My filters are going."

In the glow of the lamplight, David's wrinkles softened.

"What do you think happened to my daughter, Mr. Eager?"

A dark cloud seemed to pass over his craggy face. "I don't know. But sometimes, I get the feeling she's still in the forest. Waiting."

Lori's hands tightened on the arms of her chair. "What do you mean?"

"Sometimes, I think I see her, like she's trying to reach out to me." He pressed his fists into his eyes. "It's enough to make me question my sanity. Like last night, with all the mushrooms. But you said you didn't see anything, so it must just be me. Sometimes, it's hard to tell what's real and what's not."

The conversation had just started, but it felt like it was already spiraling out of control. David's dementia might have been playing tricks on him, but Lori couldn't ignore the possibility he was deliberately trying to mislead her. Either way, she needed to uncover as much as she could.

"Can you tell me about the day she came to visit you, Mr. Eager?"

Over steaming mugs of rich, dark coffee and a plate of gingersnap cookies, he told her about meeting Maria. He didn't reveal any new information, but what he shared intensified her feelings of remorse. Lori wished she'd known Maria better.

"She said she was off to meet an expert on mushrooms. When she didn't come back, I got worried," he said. "I called my farm manager, Bill, and we rounded up a group of people to look for her, but it was already dark, and after one of the guys sprained an ankle during the search, we decided to call the ranger."

Lori nodded. According to a newspaper account, the mushroom expert had been questioned by the police and said he last saw her at the southern entrance to the forest. He had offered to give her a ride back to Mendocino Wellness Haven, but she had declined, saying she preferred to walk.

"I've often wondered if that expert might be behind all this, the weird stuff with the mushrooms." His eyebrows lowered. "If you talk to him, I'd be careful."

Anita emerged from the kitchen and started clearing away the plates. "Oh, Mr. David, you're not talking about mushrooms again, are you?"

David shot her a dark look. "You couldn't sound more condescending if you tried, Anita." The indulgence in his voice betrayed the sternness of his expression.

There wasn't much more information to be gleaned from the man. David Eager had spent less than three hours with her daughter. Maria had checked into Cabin No. 6 but never slept there. The police had retrieved Maria's backpack and found nothing of significance inside. It had been returned to her adoptive mother. David had trouble walking, let alone anything more physical. It didn't seem likely he had harmed Maria. But he was rich. Rich people often paid people to do their dirty work. David didn't seem like a serial killer. Then again, neither had Ted Bundy.

Still, her meeting with David Eager wasn't a complete waste of time. She had discovered her daughter possessed the ability to persuade a famous recluse to speak on the record for the first time in decades and offer her a cabin for the night. He'd also described her as being empathic.

That surprised Lori. How had her aunt Erika, who was harshly judgmental, managed to raise Maria to be so charming? And thinking of her daughter as empathetic cast their relationship in a new light. It explained why Maria had seemed more interested in listening than talking about herself—something Lori had interpreted as distancing behavior. Now their past interactions felt less hurtful.

She knew who she had to see next. Julian.

But first, she needed to use the restroom.

David seemed drained after their brief meeting. He sat slumped in his chair, gazing into the crackling fire. She excused herself and followed Anita's directions to the guest bathroom at the end of the hallway. On her way back, she passed a room with a slightly open door.

Curious, she nudged it and peeked inside. David's bedroom. Lori guessed it had once been an office. Shelves covered an entire wall, filled with books and Celtic figurines carved from wood.

A window was open, letting in the chilly outside air. Something was growing on the wooden sill. It seemed to be moving. Swaying in the wind.

Lori's pulse quickened as she approached the window.

When she got closer, she could see a cluster of mushrooms growing from damp plaster around the frame. The caps were a gray-brown, frayed at the edges, their stalks white and glossy. Lori reached out to touch one. It felt wet and slippery. The moist patch on the wall spread downward to the floor, where a group of small golden umbrellas had begun to grow along the edge of the molding.

It seemed David Eager had a fungal problem after all.

Chapter 9

Amy's eyes flicked toward the small audio recorder resting on the seat beside her. It was just like Maria to turn up her nose at the equipment given to new reporters at the radio station and instead buy the expensive device used by the networks.

Maria had always had money. In San Francisco, the radio station's lousy starting salary had meant Amy lived in a shithole with roommates and surviving on cheap food. She had enjoyed Maria's generosity when they lived together— Maria had shared her apartment and her food without hesitation.

Unlike Maria, Amy hadn't gotten any help from her working-class parents. She struggled to get scholarships and financial aid, worked weekends and summers, and saved every penny. Maria could afford to take an unpaid internship at the radio station. And when she graduated, the station had offered her a job.

Amy had to start in a much smaller town and work her way up to San Francisco. She couldn't help but feel resentful.

But she was alive. Who knew what had happened to Maria?

Well, Amy could guess. Maria fell for the sad eyes of some charming stranger in Nils Forest? Maybe she went off to lend a helping hand and found herself in the back of a van. Maria was a sucker for tales of hardship. It's what had led her to specialize in human interest stories, the ones that tugged at your heart. The ones that had gotten her a job in San Francisco.

After Maria disappeared, her job had opened up. Amy applied for it and got it.

"Why don't you move back into the flat?" Erika Hart had said. "It's in Maria's name, so we won't be selling it anytime soon. At least, not until we find out for sure what happened."

Amy knew who owned the flat, and she knew who would inherit it if something happened to Maria, but there was no need for her to talk about that with Erika.

Maria's adoptive mother had said it would be too traumatic to sort through her daughter's things, so she gave everything to Amy. Which was how Amy had come into possession of fancy linens, luxurious towels, and a closet full of the gorgeous clothes she'd once envied. Except for the pants, which were too short for her tall, angular frame, she owned them all now.

As she did the small stone mushroom man Amy had found on Maria's nightstand. Amy thought the statue was creepy, but Maria had loved it. She'd gone on and on about how she'd found it on a dusty shelf at the back of a Mexican import store and suspected it dated back to the 1500s.

Maria didn't talk much about her birth mother, but she wouldn't shut up about how she could trace her bloodline through her birth father, all the way back to the Aztec Empire, and that her great grandfather had been a famous brujo and medicine man. The mushroom statue had something to do with shamans and rituals, but Amy found it all incredibly boring.

On a whim, Amy had shoved the statue into her bag, and her fingers bumped against the rough stone when she fished out Maria's digital recorder.

The buttons and the display were too small, so she could see how people might accidentally delete files. The device itself was fragile. One bump and it would probably fall apart.

In Amy's opinion, it was unsuitable for fieldwork. Of course, Maria had adored it.

"I can stick it in my pocket and go," Maria had gushed. "And the sound quality is amazing."

Amy stopped at a coffee shop in Bodega Bay, feeling the wind whip through her short hair. She had cut it recently for convenience, but now her ears were exposed to the air. Amy pulled on a beanie to keep warm. She sat at a picnic table overlooking the gray water, sipped her coffee, and examined the tiny machine. Amy didn't need an instruction booklet—she had a knack for technology. Her college professors had praised her as "tech savvy" and often asked for her help with equipment troubles. It was the one advantage she had over Maria.

The coffee scorched her tongue. She popped off the lid to let it cool, picked up the recorder, and pressed the power button with the tip of her finger. The small screen came to life.

With a tap of another button, a list of audio files appeared on the screen. There were four in total: "Notes 1," "Notes 2," "Notes 3," and "Notes 4." The police had already listened to them and determined they were of no help; they were simply observations about work and personal matters.

If Amy was being honest, she was more interested in the personal stuff. Maria had rarely talked about her private affairs. Just that she grew up with Erika, a single mother who owned a yoga studio. No explanation about how her family could have afforded to make her life so cushy or why the financial support continued after Maria graduated from college and got a job.

Amy sipped her coffee and gazed out at the bay, a small joyless smile creeping across her lips. She was determined to find Maria Hart. Or her body.

The body of the one person she'd grown to resent more than anyone else in the world.

Chapter 10

Maria's recorder didn't have a built-in speaker, which made it even more worthless. With a sigh of frustration, Amy pulled on her headphones and pressed the play button on the tiny device.

Maria's voice filled her ears.

"Okay, here we go. My therapist wants me to keep a journal to track my thoughts about my adoption, but my hand cramps up when I write a lot, so I'm doing it this way. Besides, it's easier to delete an audio file than get rid of a written journal. I'd hate it if someone besides my therapist heard these."

That made Amy smile.

Maria hadn't had many friends—no close ones as far as Amy knew—and she'd never really talked about herself. But she had opened up to the fancy little recorder and let her thoughts and feelings spill out. Which was more than a little pathetic.

Over the next few miles, Amy learned Erika Hart was Maria's adoptive mother but also her great aunt. Maria's biological mother was Lori Chambers, who became pregnant at seventeen after meeting a guy on her summer vacation in Mendocino.

Oops.

Lori Chambers had signed the baby over to her childless aunt and never looked back, at least not until years later. She had tried to get to know her daughter when Maria was in college, and they met for coffee a couple of times, but Maria wasn't very interested.

Maria was fascinated by her father, though.

"*He's Mexican. Indigenous, from Mexico. Lori said he was really into the history of Mexico before the Spanish invaded and that he could trace his ancestors all the way back to the Aztecs. She said my father's grandfather was a famous brujo in Mexico and that he came from a long line of brujos, so I am beyond excited because that means those are my ancestors too. My blood. Which is totally amazing because some people have asked if I'm Mexican or something because of the way I look, and all I could do is say I don't know because Erika said she didn't know anything about my birth father, which was a complete lie.*"

It had been Maria's father who drew her to Mendocino. He owned a bison ranch outside of the small town, and Maria wanted to meet him.

Amy wondered if Maria's plan had succeeded before she vanished. The police would know. None of the media coverage had mentioned Maria's adoption or any details about her biological family. Amy made a mental note to add Julian Cruz to her to-do list.

She'd be busy. If she wanted to avoid her assignment editor's constant pestering, she needed to investigate the reports of people getting sick in Nils Forest and grab an interview with the nurse she'd spoken to over the phone earlier. But there were so many other things…

Amy pulled off the headphones and tossed them on the passenger seat.

She had to give Maria credit—the chick knew how to keep a secret.

Chapter 11

David sat on the porch with a woolen blanket draped over his shoulders, sipping a glass of red wine he had no business drinking, given the medication he was on. But life was too short.

Correction—*his* life was too short to give up one of the few pleasures left to him. So what if it made his symptoms a little worse, the hallucinations a little more disturbing?

With a nice glass of wine at his side instead of an old man's pill bottles, he could pretend everything was normal. He'd become very good at pretending. Pretending he didn't sense something in Nils Forest had changed.

The Mexican workers, who once used a shortcut through the woods to get home, now steered clear of it, according to Bill. Something to do with the mushrooms that seemed to proliferate after the storm. David tried to question them himself, but his Spanish wasn't good enough. Neither was their English.

And now Maria's mother had shown up, bombarding him with questions. Her skin was smooth for a woman of her age, with freckles sprinkled across her nose. She had an athletic build, and she radiated good health. But there was an underlying jumpiness to her energy which set him on edge.

She'd reconnected with her daughter in Maria's final year at college. And then, just as they were getting to know each other, Maria had disappeared.

It was a strange and sad story, but it didn't have anything to do with him. He'd only met Maria hours before she vanished, yet their brief encounter seemed to have tethered him to the young woman, and now complete strangers were looking to him for answers and guidance.

Lori Chambers had departed with her shoulders hunched in disappointment, and he resented the way that made him feel. Guilty. As if he had let her down, when he had shared what little information he knew.

Of course, he'd said nothing about Maria flying above the trees on the other side of the clearing. That would have been heartless and cruel.

Despite the setting sun and the chilly air, he was determined to remain outside, if only to prove to himself all was normal and there was nothing to fear from the forest. He rapped his cane on the balcony railing and called for Anita. She appeared a few moments later, hands covered in flour.

"Can you top me up, Anita?"

She tilted her head to the side and pursed her lips, like she'd never heard the term before. He knew she was just pretending. She didn't approve of his drinking since his diagnosis.

"Anita," he said in a warning voice.

She put her hands on her hips and sighed loudly. "Okay, Mr. David. But you know that's against doctor's orders."

The screen door banged shut behind her.

"I'm sick of doctors," David muttered.

He'd finished his second glass of pinot noir when a movement near the trailhead caught his attention. A shape came hurtling out of the woods. In the dim light of dusk, it took a few seconds to resolve into a dog. Some sort of shepherd. When it reached the middle of the field, it suddenly stopped, as if surprised to find itself there.

It had something in its mouth. A tree branch, maybe.

Dogs weren't allowed off-leash in Nils Forest, but owners were known to let them run free in the woods anyway. Sometimes, they ended up at David's house, lost.

"Hey, you," he called. "It's okay. Come over here and let me take a look at your collar."

The dog's head swiveled toward him—almost guiltily, David thought.

David leaned forward, squinting, trying to make out what it was carrying.

"Come on," David called again. "Let's see what you got there."

The dog cautiously approached. When it was close enough, David could finally make out what was in its mouth.

A human arm.

It was severed just above a bloody stump of elbow and appeared to be covered in white threads. The same kind of fungal mat snaking out of the forest and covering the tiller.

A wave of revulsion rose in David's throat. When a cry escaped his mouth and he recoiled, the dog whimpered, turned around, and raced back into the forest with its find.

The screen door creaked open. Anita said, "Did you call me, Mr. David? I had the radio on."

"Did you see that dog, Anita?" David asked, scanning the expanse of trees.

Anita stepped out onto the porch, a dish towel in her hands. "No, I didn't see a dog. Was it lost? You want me to go see if I can find it?"

David pressed a finger between his eyes and shook his head.

Maybe he shouldn't have had the wine after all.

Chapter 12

Lori approached the bison farm, every muscle in her body twitching and quivering. She paused at the entrance to a winding dirt driveway. The sign read: "Cruz Bison Ranch." A giant shaggy head with horns had been carved into the wood.

She could turn around. Pack up her things at the house and head back to San Francisco, where her job, a sick mother, and adult responsibilities were waiting for her. She wanted Julian's help. But did she *need* it? Really? What could he possibly do? He was a rancher, not a private detective, and he didn't even know Maria.

Maybe Lori just wanted an excuse to see him again after all these years. Just out of sheer curiosity, wondering what kind of man he had become. What kind of man she had left. He'd had no role in Maria's life. Never knew about the decision Lori's parents had forced on her, the immense pressure to do their bidding.

And now Lori was showing up, unannounced, to ask for his help.

Her trembling fingers gripped the steering wheel, her foot pressing down on the gas pedal. The truck jumped forward.

The dirt road led past several fields filled with large animals leisurely grazing on lush green grass. In the distance, trees dotted the tops of small hills, adding to the picturesque landscape.

Her heart skipped a beat when she saw a man unloading bales of hay from a truck parked on the side of the road, dressed in a cowboy hat and jeans. But he was too young and too tall to be Julian. The man gave her a friendly wave when she drove past him.

Lori followed the road until it ended at a two-story house made of weathered wooden shingles. A newer, more modern building stood next to it, with plenty of windows and corrugated steel walls. On the door, stenciled lettering read: "Cruz Bison Ranch Store." The bright green neon sign above it indicated it was open.

She sat in the truck for a few moments, her eyes darting nervously toward the door, half expecting someone to come out and investigate. And sure enough, as if she'd willed it, the door opened and a man stepped out.

It was Julian. All the soft edges of youth had been replaced by sharp angles. But his smooth brown skin remained, along with his regal nose—the same nose Maria had inherited.

He leaned down, craning his neck to peer inside her truck.

Lori's mouth had gone dry. She swallowed hard before getting out of the vehicle. Julian looked up.

"Hey." Her voice sounded distant, unfamiliar.

Julian stared at her blankly. Her heart sank. He didn't recognize her. Had she changed that much? By the expression on his face, she had.

"It's me. Lori."

Julian opened his mouth to speak, then closed it. After a long silence, he said, "Hey yourself." He crossed his arms over his chest, a frown forming on his handsome face. "What are you doing here?" He paused. "Is there news? About Maria?"

Lori's legs grew weak, and she had to lean against the truck for support. She shook her head. "No. There's nothing."

A deep furrow formed between his eyebrows. "Then why are you here?"

"The police aren't doing enough to find her," she blurted out. "I think we should do something. I think we should look for her ourselves."

"We?" Julian exploded. "Are you serious? I haven't heard from you in how long? Twenty-seven years?" His voice rose. "In case you forgot, you never bothered to tell me I had a daughter, and then when she went missing, you didn't bother to tell me that either. Jesus H. Christ, Lori. I had to find out everything from the police when they came to question me. Do you have any idea how that felt?"

Julian's voice broke, and he fought back tears.

"She wanted to meet me! I had no clue she even existed. You broke up with me. No explanation. Just said you couldn't see me again. Do you have any idea how that messed me up? Didn't you think I would have wanted to be there for you, for our *child*? But you never gave me that choice, and now you're here? Expecting me to do what, exactly?"

Lori twisted her hands together and met his furious gaze. She tried to find the right words, any words, to explain the rollercoaster she'd been on since finding out she was pregnant, but they eluded her.

"I—" Her voice faltered. The conversation was moving too fast into deep and unfamiliar territory.

Julian shook his head in disbelief and took a few steps back, pacing on the steps leading to the store. "Madre mia de Dios, Lori. She's been gone for six months. You finally decide to show up out of the blue? To do what? Play Nancy Drew?"

Lori raised a shaking hand to cut him off. "It's not completely out of the blue. You must have heard. Four other people have disappeared in Nils Forest, and the police are out searching for the most recent one. This is our chance to remind them Maria is still missing and they can't give up trying to find her just because it's been a while. She's become a cold case and they've stopped trying!"

Julian tilted his head back and groaned. "Why would they even listen to us, Lori? We have no legal standing. You signed away our daughter. What about the woman who raised her? What is *she* doing?"

Lori choked back a sob. "Nothing. My aunt is convinced that Maria is gone. Murdered. She says we have to prepare for the worst and accept whatever has happened. But I can't, Julian. I'm sorry for what I did back then. It wasn't fair to you. But my parents forced me to do it. They were…"

Julian snorted. "Racist."

"They *were* racist." The words came out as a whisper.

Julian let out a bitter laugh. "Ha! There. You finally said it. I knew it from the first time I met them. Man, the look on their faces when they caught us together in town. If you'd hooked up with a white blueblood, things would have turned out very differently. There's no way the high and mighty Chambers family wanted a Mexican involved with their daughter, and I'm guessing they sure as hell didn't want a brown grandchild. That's what it was all about, right? Not them thinking you were too young to raise a baby, with all the money they have. Because they couldn't stand a baby that looked more like my people than yours."

Lori leaned against the truck, suddenly exhausted. Julian had guessed the awful truth. "They were—*are*—racist and controlling and spiteful. But I depended on them for everything. I had no choice."

Her parents had demanded she break off her relationship with Julian, then that she give up her child so her aunt could adopt Maria. Lori's father hadn't wanted to involve any outsiders, fearing people would find out his daughter was an unwed, teenage mother who had slept with a Mexican farmhand. Lori had gone along with it. She'd never much cared for self-centered Erika, but at least she wouldn't lose track of her daughter.

The baby had striking dark eyes and a head full of fuzzy dark hair. Lori thought she was beautiful, like Julian. Her parents, however, had turned away. The irony was, Maria's hair lightened as she got older, but it was no matter.

Julian sat down on the top step and covered his face with his hands. He remained in that position for what felt like an eternity. When he raised his head, his eyes glistened with tears. "I can't tell you how that felt, you know? You not even bothering to tell me I had a kid. My wife left me because she didn't want kids. But I did. I would have loved to know Maria, and it kills me that I never got that chance."

He sounded lost. Like the days when she had first met him, when he was fighting his family's demands to stay on the farm instead of going away to college. An only son's duty, they'd said. Lori remembered how she used to comfort him during those times, especially when they were alone in Nils Forest.

"I'm sorry," she said softly, fighting the urge to go to him and wrap her arms around his neck like she once had.

Julian's head dropped. He sniffled and wiped away the tears with the backs of his hands. "Yeah. Okay." He paused, staring into the distance. "Let's be realistic, Lori. What can we do? What can we do that the police haven't already done? Unless there's something you know that I don't."

Seeing the longing and anticipation in his eyes made her want to cry. "Unfortunately, I don't. But I do have an idea where we can look."

Chapter 13

Julian heard her out, a sour expression on his face the entire time, then immediately began shaking his head. They'd moved into the market and sat at a table in the front.

"The search teams would have already looked in the lime kilns." His tone was crisp and businesslike.

She shrugged. "Maybe they did. But it's possible they didn't know about the room *behind* the kilns. The one we found."

The one where they'd hidden from the world, from their parents, and from their problems. The place where Maria had been conceived.

They talked for an hour, their conversation leapfrogging from past to present and back again, trying to stitch together the lost threads of their lives. It took a while for Julian to stop bringing up how much she'd hurt him, of how much life damage she'd done. To them all.

"I know, I know," she finally cried. "But I was just a kid. My parents threatened to cut me off. I should have stood up to them. I tried, but I wasn't strong enough. You have no idea what they can be like. And they kept saying it was for my own good, and that if I kept her, it would ruin my life."

Julian pursed his lips and looked away. When he finally turned back to face her, his voice was gruff. "Yeah. You were just a kid. We both were." He hesitated. "I'm sorry you had to go through all that alone, but couldn't you have called me? We could have talked it through. Tried to figure it out, together."

Decades of regret washed over her. "I should have. But if my parents had cut me off..." Lori sighed.

She felt like a fool for ending it with Julian. But she hadn't been herself, didn't feel like she had any options. Lori just did what she was told to do. And she was still under her father's thumb, working for his commercial real estate business. The vulnerable teenager who had lost her daughter was never far from the surface, even at her age.

There had never been anyone like Julian. She'd had relationships, but none had ever worked, especially a disastrous marriage lasting less than a year.

Julian got up and went behind the counter. "I'm making some coffee."

She nodded absently, distracted by a row of photos on the wall, and went over to take a look.

In one, Julian was standing next to a pretty, petite woman with dark hair, a herd of buffalo behind him. Julian's ex-wife, she guessed. There was one of Julian with his parents, another with his ranch hands, and several with Julian and a group of young teenagers.

"Who are these kids?" she asked.

Julian looked up from spooning coffee out of a tin, a swoop of black hair falling over his forehead. "We've got a lot of migrant workers in the county. I started a summer program for them. It's run with the help of the community college. They take English classes there and learn about going to college. Then they come here and learn how to start a business—basic stuff, like what it takes to operate a ranch and a store like this one. We do a lot of barbequing and just hanging out too. I try to make it fun."

Lori turned to stare at him. "You're kidding."

"I am not." He chuckled, as if amused she was so surprised.

And she was. Another photo caught her attention. This one of Julian talking into a microphone, seated behind a large dais. She tapped the silver frame. "What's going on here?"

Julian laughed again. "You're not going to believe this, but the doofus you dated in high school is on the city council."

It was hard to take it all in. Julian had changed. A lot. From a quiet teenager filled with doubt to this confident, take-charge man. She'd missed out on so much. There was one more photo, smaller than the others. A faded black and white snapshot showing a small group of people in an overgrown garden, the man closest to the camera holding up what looked like a ceramic bowl, smoke rising into the air. Julian's grandfather, she guessed. The famous Mexican brujo. His hair was slicked back, his mouth slightly open and his eyes closed. Behind him stood a beautiful young woman wearing a ruffled dress, with a high-bridged nose and a wide mouth.

She looked exactly like Maria. The way she was staring directly at the camera made Lori's neck tingle.

Pulse quickening, she snatched the photo from the wall and held it up to Julian, who was pouring coffee into mugs. "Who is this? An aunt?"

Julian glanced up and squinted at the photo, head flinching back slightly. "I don't know. That's weird. I've never seen her before."

"What do you mean? You must have hung the photo on the wall, right? You didn't notice her? She's kind of hard to miss." There was something about the woman in the photo that commanded attention. The intensity of her gaze, perhaps, or her youth and beauty.

Julian continued to stare at the image, shaking his head. "No. What I'm saying is, I've never seen her before because she wasn't there. Ever. That picture's been around for as long

61

as I can remember. I put it up after I finally finished clearing out my parent's house last year."

Lori tapped the frame. "Then how do you explain this? Because she's a dead ringer for Maria. I mean, it could actually be her."

"I can't explain it, but I'm telling you, the girl wasn't there before. If my mother was still alive, she'd say my grandfather was up to his old tricks. He was a bit of a prankster. My mother used to swear he gave his neighbor's dog two tails because it would chase their chickens."

"But your grandfather's dead," Lori protested. "Isn't there anybody else in your family who can…"—she searched for the right word—"…do stuff like that?"

Julian walked around the counter and set two mugs on the table. "I've heard that one of my older cousins has the gift. A brujo in his own right. But I haven't talked to him in years, and he doesn't know that I have a daughter."

Lori went back to gazing at the photo. The woman stared back. "I can't get over how much she looks like Maria."

Julian took the picture from her hands, went behind the counter, wrapped it in butcher paper, then shoved it in a drawer.

"What are you doing?"

"There's something wrong with that picture," he said, voice hoarse. "And since it's not likely I'm going to figure it out anytime soon, I'm not comfortable with having it out."

Lori sank into her chair and sipped her coffee. She wouldn't have minded something stronger, but it was still early in the day, and she didn't want to look like she had a drinking problem. Her thoughts kept returning to the young woman in the photo.

She couldn't shake the feeling that the woman *was* Maria, but it wasn't anything she could say to Julian. He already thought she was crazy enough for showing up unannounced, asking for his help to find the daughter she'd kept secret from him. It was a miracle he was even speaking to her.

Lori sat quietly, allowing him to brood in silence while he drank his coffee.

Finally, he set down his mug and cleared his throat. "You said you talked to the police chief? Did you ask if they searched the kilns?"

She placed her mug on the table. "No. But they must have. It's the perfect place to hide a..." Her words trailed off, and a cough erupted from her throat.

Body. The perfect place to hide a body.

Instead of berating the chief, she could have mentioned the hidden room.

The forest was vast, and the kilns were notoriously difficult to find, known only to seasoned hikers and brave adventurers. Regardless of which entrance one used, it took hours to reach them. Julian had learned about the kilns from a friend, and their first excursion had taken an entire day, starting just after dawn.

"We should tell the police," Julian said firmly. "How long did it take for us to find that back room?"

Lori thought for a moment. She suppressed a smile, remembering what they'd done when they finally found it. "At least three trips."

"Did they use search dogs? If they had dogs, they would have discovered anyone back there."

Lori shrugged, shoulders slumping. "I assume so." She was tired of waiting for others to find her missing daughter. It wasn't complicated—they could search the forest and the kilns themselves. If they stumbled on something significant, they'd alert the authorities. At the very least, it was something to do to make her feel useful.

Lori reached across the table and took hold of Julian's hand. "Please. Please, Julian. Let's take a look."

He gazed down at their joined hands, eyebrows knitting together. "I heard the search crew got sick in the forest and had to go to the hospital. What's that about?"

"I don't know. That's news to me."

"You and I never got sick, and we used to go there all the time. Maybe we're immune from whatever it is."

"Maybe. But Julian, what if the searchers never even made it to the kilns because they got sick and turned back? That's not something the police chief would want to admit, right?" It was a bit of a stretch but possible. And she needed to convince Julian to help her.

His expression turned dark. "They must have checked." His eyes widened. "Wait. An employee of mine is friends with one of the searchers who got sick. That's how I heard about it." He grabbed his phone. Moments later, Lori heard him make the request. "Yeah, long story, but can you text me his number? There are some questions I want to ask him."

As soon as he hung up, a chime signaled a text arrival. Julian punched the number into his phone. His excitement was palpable, like an electric charge in the air.

"I know, I know, but yeah. I'm her biological father. No, we were supposed to meet before she disappeared." He leaned in, elbows on the table, listening intently while the man on the other end of the line spoke.

Lori couldn't make out the words, but she could sense agitation from his tone.

After they ended the call, Julian rubbed the side of his face, frowning slightly. "That was one of the guys from the search team. He said they checked the kilns after Maria went missing, and again after two of the others disappeared, but not since then. He said it's like a big part of the forest has become off-limits, with wild theories going around about what could be making people sick. He said the ranger thinks it's all a crock of shit, and the police chief won't touch it either because the last thing they need is for people to start panicking about aliens or Bigfoot in the forest."

Lori pressed a hand to the side of her head. Her temples throbbed. "Did he know about the room behind the kilns?"

"No. It was news to him." Julian got up and looked out the window.

She couldn't see his expression. His hair was still thick and glossy as a raven's feathers, but now it was shot through with silver strands. He wasn't tall, but he had a strong, compact build which could only come from long hours at a gym or manual labor on a ranch. Or both. When he finally turned to face her, there was tension in his jaw.

"I don't know what's happening in the forest, Lor, but something's off. And you're right. We need to search the kilns ourselves."

At hearing her old nickname, Lori's pulse quickened, a blend of excitement and apprehension flooding her veins. The chances were slim their daughter was still alive, but Lori held onto the hope that, by taking matters into their own hands, they might find out what had happened to Maria.

Chapter 14

David's eyes fluttered open, his heart already racing before he was fully awake. Nightmares blended into reality with increasing frequency, but he hadn't completely lost it yet. He could still distinguish between what was real and what wasn't. Even in the grip of his hallucinations, he usually managed to stay separate from them, an observer from a distance with his rational mind still intact. His neurologist was fascinated by his descriptions of his descent into Lewy body dementia, and while the doctor didn't explicitly say it, by the questions he asked and the puzzled expressions he wore when he listened to David's answers, David had the sense his disease was progressing in an unusual way.

Someone was screaming outside in the darkness. A piercing shriek coming from the nearby forest.

With some effort, David propped himself up on one elbow and glanced at the open casement window. He was certain he had closed and latched it before going to bed. The window creaked in the wind, but he didn't want to look out for fear of seeing the flying woman again. She might be there now, waiting for him.

The wind was howling through the trees. That's what he must have heard. The wind. Not screaming.

But then, words rode in on a gust, banging the window against the exterior wall.

"Help! Help!"

Maybe it was Karl Ackerman stumbling out of the woods, injured but finally returning after getting lost in the endless expanse of trees.

David had only been able to explore a small portion of the forest before his body began to deteriorate. But he knew it was massive, passing through a series of hills and a mountain range before ending at the Pacific Ocean.

If it was Karl, he needed help. Faster than David was capable of moving.

His overnight caretaker slept in a room at the back of the house and was unlikely to have heard the shrieks coming from the trees.

"Andrea!" he yelled. And waited.

But there was only the howling wind. Another cry echoed from outside, fainter this time and more distant.

Maybe it wasn't Andrea's turn to stay over. Maybe it was Stuart, the bald man with the tattoos. Stuart had such good hearing, sometimes David suspected he'd placed a baby monitor in his room. Anytime David stirred, Stuart would appear.

And then he remembered. He'd sent Andrea home. She'd crossed a boundary, entered the bathroom while he was bathing in the chair made for invalids. It was an unforgivable violation which left him feeling powerless and robbed him of his dignity.

Now, he was alone in the empty house.

The windows shook in their frames, the cries for help thinning into an unrelenting wail making him want to hide under the covers and block out the noise. But he couldn't give in to fear. His illness was no excuse for cowardice. If it *was* Karl outside, he needed help, and there was no one else to provide it.

David slid his legs off the bed and reached for his walker. The cold floor sent a sharp chill through his bare feet. He ignored his orthopedic slippers. Despite the physical therapist's recommendation that he wear them at all times when he was indoors, he found he didn't need them anymore.

In fact, since the fungal outbreak in his home, he'd noticed an improvement in his ability to walk. David had kept this to himself. There was no point mentioning it to anyone, not even his doctor or Wellness Haven's manager. She'd discovered the mushrooms growing on his windowsill and had called in a specialist to get rid of them.

But as soon as the fungus had been removed, David's feet began to ache again, and his awkward, labored gait returned. When new clusters of mushrooms appeared behind his headboard and in his closet, David said nothing. It might have been irrational, superstitious even, but he couldn't help but connect the mushrooms with his improved motor skills.

He retrieved a flashlight from the nightstand's top drawer and made his way into the hallway.

His bedroom door slammed shut behind him, blown by the wind. He gave a violent start, his hands spasming on his walker.

When he reached the living room, he realized he was walking with more ease than he'd experienced in a while. A smile of astonishment spread across his face at the simple pleasure of being able to walk. Step by step, his brain sent the necessary commands to his legs.

You're not out for a stroll, he scolded himself sternly. Someone needed help. He had to focus.

He crossed the living room in slow but confident strides and turned on a floor lamp, casting a warm glow on the walls around the front door.

The walls. Something strange had happened to the walls.

A web of white fibers covered the wood panels, clustering in places to create lumpy masses. They appeared to have a pulsing life of their own. The network of fibers seemed densest near the door, and at some intersections, mushroom caps sprouted. Each cap was a different shape and color—white, orange, yellow, green, purple. And the textures varied too: smooth, ragged and split-edged, and even hairy.

This time, he was sure he wasn't imagining things.

For a moment, the commotion outside receded. David reached out, his fingers stopping just inches away from the pulsating, living wall. In the lamplight, he noticed his hand was surprisingly steady. His finger grazed a funnel-shaped mushroom, its color an unusual shade of dark orange. The delicate edges crinkled, as if startled by his touch.

David shuddered, then took in the blend of earthy scents in the room and wondered where they had come from, these strange mushrooms taking over his walls.

A cluster of white mounds jutted out from the door frame. The mushrooms didn't have stalks like the others and were slightly larger than golf balls. Memories flooded back to him from his childhood, when he would visit his cousins at the end of summer break. They used to play together in the field behind their house, and one of their favorite games was stomping on round, soft mushrooms, causing them to release a magical cloud of spores. His aunt had called them "puffballs."

Without thinking, he struck the nearest one. It collapsed under his touch.

A burst of powdery particles exploded in the air, hitting him square in the face. He coughed, then sneezed and sputtered. His head felt as weightless and insubstantial as a dandelion. His body swayed back and forth, and for a moment, he feared he might fall over. But he managed to steady himself. David looked down at his feet in amazement. Growing between two wooden planks was a dark mushroom with an impossibly thin stem, almost as high as his knees.

He reached down and gently picked it, like one would gather a delicate flower. David took a moment to study it, realizing what he had just accomplished. He had bent over without hesitation or difficulty—something that had been impossible for a long, long time.

But he was distracted again. If Karl Ackerman was out there, David was determined to find him, even if it meant venturing into the dark and braving the expanse of meadow without his walker. He flung open the door. The wind had stopped. Not even a breeze stirred treetops. It was eerily quiet.

"Karl!" he shouted into the darkness. His own voice sounded unfamiliar—clear, strong.

Silence greeted him.

When he called again, laughter came from the edge of the forest. A woman's laugh, resonant and triumphant, echoed through the trees

.

Chapter 15

David returned to his room and climbed into bed. He stared at the ceiling, trying to make sense of what had just happened. Were the mushrooms in his living room real? Had he actually heard a voice in the forest? Had his motor skills improved? Or were all of these things in his head, products of his disease mingling with his irrational hope he might somehow pull out of the spiral of his dementia?

He closed his eyes and tried to go back to sleep.

From the darkest corner of his bedroom, David heard the unmistakable sound of someone whispering. He covered his ears to shut it out. No one else was in the room, not at this hour. None of his caretakers would dare enter, not without knocking first. They knew that would cost them their jobs.

The whispers continued, becoming clearer. It sounded like someone was chanting.

David's body quivered. He propped himself up on one elbow and peered into the dark room. In the faint light coming from the bathroom, he could just make out a figure in the corner, back pressed against the wall, a hand raised in the air.

He should have been afraid. His heart was beating fast, but more from surprise than fear. His head felt funny, thick, and his thoughts were fuzzy. It was as if he'd emerged from a deep slumber, disoriented and groggy. Had he been in the hospital? Was he waking for the first time after a procedure he couldn't remember?

"Nurse?"

The whispering stopped, and the figure shifted slightly. After a long silence, a woman's voice, slightly husky, "Be well, David."

"Who are you?" He squinted into the darkness. "What are you doing in my room?"

"Don't worry. Everything is going to be all right. I want you to remember that." The woman's voice held a hint of concern.

The whispered chanting began again.

Enough of this nonsense, David decided. Time to get this crazy woman out of his house.

But something rustled behind him, and something slithered along the nape of his neck, like a hundred tiny, crawling insects. He tried to brush them away. Not bugs, but threads snaking across his skin, tightening their grip as they slid through his hair, then crawled down his forehead. Falling back on the bed, he clawed at the grotesque web spreading across his face.

The strands were tough and fibrous. He managed to pull them away a few inches before they snapped back into place, tighter than before. The filaments divided and connected at the same time, forming a mesh covering his cheeks and nose, inching toward his mouth. He screamed.

The figure had moved to the foot of his bed, both hands raised in the air, its whispered incantations growing louder and more urgent.

"Stop it, please!" His voice cracked. But there was nobody to help him.

Thin tendrils brushed against his lips. For one horrible moment, he thought they would enter his mouth, but in a sudden burst of motion, they engulfed his chin, and he was forced to breathe through his nose.

His entire head was enveloped now, his eyes and mouth sealed shut. The fibers continued their relentless downward creep, covering his neck and shoulders. David could feel their clammy touch, their strange scent invading his nostrils—a heady mixture of dirt, decay, and sweetness.

The mycelium. The fungal threads which had covered the tiller were consuming him, and the dark force controlling the fungus was watching.

Or was it something else? A tactile hallucination, the symptom of his dementia he'd feared the most?

David felt like he was teetering on the razor's edge of madness. He frantically tried to think objectively but felt himself being pulled slowly toward insanity.

David was paralyzed, pinned to the mattress by the sinister strands.

At least he could still breathe.

What had he done to deserve such a punishment?

The filaments continued to tighten, and a primal fear began to overtake him. He breathed in through his nose, but with each inhale came more terror. If he didn't calm down, he would surely die.

David began counting to ten, willing away his fear. *One...Two...Three...*

He'd just reached the count of eight when the threads loosened slightly. Maybe they'd only tightened in response to his struggling. David tried to relax his muscles, but his body was still in fight mode, and the most he could manage was to unclench his jaw.

How much time had passed since he'd become a prisoner of the sinister mycelium? If the woman was still in the room, he had no way of knowing it. David couldn't hear anything over the sound of his heartbeat booming in his ears.

He didn't know how much longer he could hold out, whether he'd pass out, have a heart attack, or experience a stroke.

David had to fight back.

Fingers frantically clawing at the bedsheet, heels digging into the mattress, he tried wriggling his upper body to test the strength of the filaments imprisoning him and was immediately met with a new level of horror. The web of sticky filaments began to move again, sliding back and forth in a macabre dance against his skin. A gurgle rose in his throat, a scream trapped inside his mouth.

Surely, this torture was his dementia advancing to a new, horrible stage.

The bed began to spin. White spots danced inside his closed eyes. The filaments pressed into his skin so hard, he feared they might slice him open. A sharp pain seared his right elbow. His body reacted in a violent shudder, vision blurring.

All at once, the fibers went limp. They began to retreat, pulling back toward the head of his bed, like a thousand tiny tape measures retracting into their cases. While his body was free, his ears were filled with an unsettling susurration, as if many voices were whispering all around the room.

David struggled to sit up, and the last of the white strings slipped over the side of his mattress. He panted, his eyes flicking toward the foot of his bed.

No one was there. The figure had retreated into the darkest corner of the room.

"You...," he stammered. He didn't have the energy to say more.

"Be calm." The husky voice had softened. "You're better now."

David was so exhausted, he couldn't do anything but sink back onto his pillow, shut his eyes, and take deep breaths to cleanse his mind of his ordeal.

He woke hours later, with only a fuzzy recollection of the abominable experience. David was certain he'd had a tactile hallucination. It had felt real—horribly, terribly real, and yet, he was strangely calm and rested. For once, he had slept peacefully, without being tormented by nightmares.

With a sudden burst of energy, David swung his legs off the bed and sat up, his eyes snapping open. What a difference a good night's sleep could make, he thought. He felt refreshed. David was even able to stand up and walk to the window in just three easy steps. Outside, the sun was rising, casting a golden light on the emerald-green grass in the meadow.

And then he remembered the final words spoken by the woman in his room.

You're better now.

He was. He was better.

David sat back down on the bed and took inventory. He no longer felt as though his body was failing him.

David looked down and examined his elbow. There was a razor-thin fissure about three inches long where he'd felt the filaments tighten, the flesh around it red and tender.

Hallucinations didn't slice you open, David thought. In a flash of realization, he understood.

The mycelium and the woman had been real, and they'd come to help him, not hurt him. How, he could not comprehend. But he had not felt this good, this strong, for a long time. Whatever the mycelium had done, it had worked wonders.

At least, he desperately hoped that's what had happened.

Chapter 16

Amy drove into the tiny village of Mendocino and whistled. It was every bit as charming as it appeared on *Murder, She Wrote,* an '80s TV show filmed in the seaside town.

Rows of perfectly manicured Victorian houses, a Gothic-style white church with a belltower, spectacular gardens, and rose-wrapped picket fences. The village was picture perfect.

She drove past a bookstore, galleries, restaurants, pubs, and shops. From the edge of town, she could see Mendocino Headlands State Park, with its miles of gentle trails winding among the dramatic ocean bluffs, and beyond, the steel blue waters of the Pacific Ocean. People were bundled up in coats and scarves, braving the cool autumn breezes.

Amy desperately craved a cup of coffee. Nothing fancy, just a quick jolt of caffeine. She caught sight of a market and went inside. The charm of the town stopped at the front door. Inside, the market resembled the bodegas from her hometown in New Jersey. Maybe not as cluttered, but still in need of a good cleaning.

She strode toward the counter, where a clerk with edgy, spiked hair and green eyeshadow was chatting with a man and woman. As Amy approached, their conversation came to an abrupt stop, and they turned to eye her with a blend of wariness and annoyance. She must have interrupted a juicy gossip session.

Amy went to the coffee pot on the counter and filled a paper cup. She had just finished pouring cream into her coffee when she glanced up and met the intense gaze of the man. Her hand gave an involuntary jerk of surprise, and she nearly dropped the cream dispenser. His features looked familiar. The strong nose, the high cheekbones, the almond-shaped eyes.

"Is your name Julian?" she blurted out.

The man frowned. "Have we met?"

"Julian Cruz?" Amy persisted.

He hesitated before nodding, his frown deepening. "Do I know you?"

"No. My name is Amy Matthews. I knew Maria. We were friends." She set down the carafe, coffee forgotten.

Julian stared at her. The tall woman with dirty blond hair standing next to him clutched his arm. Amy's chest tingled. If the man was Maria's father, this had to be her mother. She had Maria's wide mouth and chin. But it made no sense. According to Maria, her parents were estranged and hadn't even spoken since before her birth. Yet here they were, shopping together at the local market.

The woman was the first to regain her composure. "I'm Lori Chambers. Maria's mother..." Her voice drifted off. She cleared her throat before continuing. "Do you live here? I didn't think Maria knew anyone in Mendocino."

The clerk leaned against the counter, following the conversation like a fan watching their favorite TV show. Amy ignored him. For now.

"Just visiting. In fact, I was hoping to find you. Both of you."

She paused. Her assignment focused on the strange incidents at Nils Forest. She didn't need to speak with Maria's birth parents to do that story. But she had been hoping to meet them eventually, just to satisfy her own curiosity. So, this was a stroke of luck.

"I work at the same radio station Maria did. We were roommates. During the last year of college too. Maybe she mentioned me?"

Lori shook her head. "No, she didn't, I'm afraid." She looked like she wanted to say more but thought better of it. "Maria must have spoken about me to you."

Amy sipped her coffee, buying a few moments to consider her response. The truth was, Maria had shared almost nothing about her birth mother. Just that she had one and was trying to sort out her feelings about the woman and the situation.

"A bit," she replied cautiously. "Maria was a very private person."

She hesitated. Lori wouldn't be too happy if she knew what Maria had revealed about her on that recorder, but there was nothing Amy could do about that.

Amy continued, "But the station gave me access to Maria's old recorder. I listened to an audio diary she made on my drive up. She mentioned the both of you. Would—"

Julian jumped in. "Can we hear those recordings? Please?"

The man working behind the counter was perched on a stool, arms crossed over his narrow chest. He sported glittery green nail polish and a silver chain wrapped around his wrist. The man seemed out of place in rural Mendocino.

"You're not Eternal Goth, by any chance?" Amy asked.

The man's eyes widened. "Oh my god. Yes. That's me. Wait…You're the one who messaged me." He smacked his forehead. "I've been working so much I completely forgot to get back to you. You're Talk Bitch?"

Amy's cheeks grew warm. She'd meant to change her username when she started at the radio station but had forgotten. "Yeah. That's me. Did your friend agree to talk to me?"

Eternal Goth turned to Lori and Julian. "You're not the only ones asking questions about Nils Forest. Amy here read my posts and reached out. She wants to meet my friend at the urgent care. The same guy you were just asking about."

His nametag, Amy noted, read "Joe." He didn't look like a Joe. Eternal Goth suited him much better.

Amy's heart sank. If Lori and Julian were onto the story, how many others out there were following it? Knowing her luck, journalists would soon converge on Mendocino, and she'd lose whatever small advantage she had.

Julian glanced at Lori, then cleared his throat. "We'd like to hear that tape."

"It's a digital file," Amy automatically corrected him. "And sure, we can listen to it. But first, I need to ask Joe a few questions."

Before Joe could reply, a bell above the door clanged, and two disheveled teenagers poked their heads into the store. Joe quickly went to greet them. The three stepped outside together.

"Where are you staying?" Lori asked.

Amy shrugged. "Haven't figured that out yet. Someplace cheap. Any chance you can recommend a motel without bedbugs?"

"Why don't you stay with me?" Lori said. "I have a place nearby. We were headed there next, actually. And there's plenty of room."

"Are you serious? You barely know me."

"You're friends with my daughter. That's good enough for me."

Amy glanced at Julian, who also seemed surprised. She hoped Lori wasn't some kind of nut. But staying with her would solve all sorts of problems. Like avoiding a sketchy motel and having easy access to a source. Two sources, counting Julian.

"Thank you," she said, managing to sound suitably grateful. "I'd appreciate that."

Before they left the market, Amy took down Joe's number, along with the contact information for his urgent care friend—the one who'd treated the people getting sick in Nils Forest.

Chapter 17

If there was any question Maria had come from money, it was erased as soon as Amy pulled into the driveway. The house sat at the north edge of town, in what had to be a prime piece of real estate next to the headlands. It exuded luxury, like something straight out of one of those architectural magazines featuring unique and extravagant homes.

It wasn't enormous. In fact, it was half the size of its neighbors but also twice as nice, with dramatic angles, lots of wooden windows, and a stunning garden. There was even a tower that seemed like it had been plucked from a fairy tale.

Inside was bright and airy. The rooms on the lower level were tastefully furnished.

"My parents built this place when I was a kid." Lori pointed Amy toward a narrow flight of wooden stairs. "There are two rooms up there. Take your pick."

Amy went up the stairs, but Lori made no move to follow. Instead, she headed straight for the kitchen with Julian in tow. Judging by his wide-eyed gaze, it was his first time in the house too.

Amy chose the smaller of the two bedrooms because it came with a private bathroom. The wood furniture had a polished sheen. She ran her hand along the thick white comforter. In the bathroom, the towels were pure white and as fluffy as clouds. Pure bliss.

But the house and everything it represented filled her with burning resentment. Amy's working-class roots and constant money worries had made her sharp and brittle.

While she took in her surroundings, she could practically feel her edges hardening.

Why did her humble origins still haunt her long after escaping New Jersey? Other people had blue-collar backgrounds and crappy childhood homes and seemed to move past it.

She placed her tote bag on the desk next to the large window overlooking the side yard. A low stone wall separated the private area from an expanse of grass leading to a network of trails and, finally, a cliff. She slid open the window. The sea was a distant roar. Amy reached into her bag, and her fingers closed on the small metal recorder and her headphones. She headed back downstairs.

Lori and Julian were sitting at the dining table, a bottle of red wine between them. Three glasses. Lori silently nudged one toward her. Amy had no qualms about drinking on the job. Julian poured. Amy sipped it, relishing the warmth sliding down her throat. Smooth and delicious, but she wouldn't have expected anything else.

She cleared her throat and began. "This recorder belonged to Maria. She bought it, but the police returned it to the station. They let me borrow it, but they'll want it back. You're welcome to listen as long as you understand you won't be able to keep it."

Lori opened her mouth as if to object, but Julian patted her hand and said, "Of course, thank you. Right, Lor? That's not a problem?"

Lori rubbed her neck, hard enough a red mark emerged. "That's fine," she replied, lips pursing as if she had just tasted something sour.

Amy grabbed the headphones and inserted the jack into a port on the recorder's side. "This thing is ridiculous. You need headphones to listen to what's on it, and whatever you do, don't press any buttons because you might accidentally delete something. It's easy to do with these things. Who wants to go first?"

"There's no way for us to listen together?" Julian asked.

Without waiting for a reply, Lori snatched the headphones from her hand. Amy hit play.

Lori listened, and tears welled up in her eyes. Amy thought maybe she should get up and give the woman some space, some privacy. But instead, she pretended to be playing some sort of game on her flip phone. Julian got up and left the room, returning with a tissue box, which he set in front of Lori.

When Lori was done, she walked over to the long line of windows and gazed out at the garden. By the way her shoulders were shaking, Amy knew she was crying.

Julian sat with his arms crossed and his head lowered, listening to the voice of the daughter he had never known. When the tracks ended, he leaned back in his chair and ran a hand through his black hair.

"Lori?" His voice was rough, his eyes dull. "You told her about me."

Lori turned quickly, a hand reaching up to touch her face. "Of course I did."

"You told her my grandfather was a brujo." Julian pulled the headphones down to hang around his neck.

"That's what you said," Lori replied, voice rising.

Julian shook his head. "Of all things to tell her, you told her that?"

"You have such a rich heritage, Julian. She deserves to know about it. And it's a lot more interesting than my background."

"That mushroom expert she was supposed to meet with?" Julian asked. "Do either of you know if she met him?

The police must have questioned him, right? He was probably the last person to see her alive."

Lori's face drained of color. "You mean, the last person she saw before she disappeared, goddammit."

Julian held up two placating hands. "I'm sorry. Before she disappeared. I'm sorry. Can you call the police chief and ask what the guy said?"

Amy sighed. It was time to remind Maria's parents they weren't the only ones in the room. "Why don't we find this mushroom guy and ask him ourselves?"

The sound of Amy's voice seemed to catch Julian off guard. He sat up straight in his chair, accidentally yanking the headphone cord and pulling the recorder off the table. Amy watched in alarm as the silver device dangled precariously, slamming against a table leg. Flustered, Julian grabbed it, his fingers pressing down on the buttons.

"Shit," Amy cried.

She leaped up and grabbed the recorder, biting her bottom lip and studying the device for damage. Amy put the headphones on and found the first audio file. It was there, thank God. She flipped through the list of recordings, and only when she was done did she let out a deep breath and slump back onto her chair.

But something on the recorder's little screen caught her eye. Another folder had appeared, with several audio tracks nestled within it. Her pulse quickened.

Whatever they were about, she needed to listen to them alone.

"Did I mess it up?" Julian asked nervously.

Lori paced behind him, frowning.

"It's fine," Amy said lightly. "If you don't mind, I'm going to go upstairs and do a little work."

Without waiting for a reply, Amy put the recorder in her tote and ran upstairs.

Debra Castaneda

Chapter 18

Lori woke, head pounding. She'd drank too much wine after Julian left. Two glasses in, she'd invited him to stay, but he'd refused. The memory of his shocked expression seemed to make her hangover worse. Amy was bustling in the kitchen, the aroma of toast and coffee filling the air.

She needed coffee. Lots of it, and water too. Lori tugged on a pair of sweatpants and padded into the kitchen. No need for slippers in the Mendocino house—it had electric heating under the floors.

Amy was rooting around in the refrigerator, her back turned, giving Lori time to study the young woman. Tall and thin with impossibly long legs, she resembled a stork. When she saw Lori, Amy flashed a shy, somewhat crooked smile. It was a face that should not have been beautiful but was, with large, buggy eyes set in a narrow face, odd features accentuated by an unflattering haircut—chopped straight across, just below the ears. She had already showered and dressed for the day.

"Good morning," Lori announced. Her voice echoed through the quiet room. She crossed to the sink and filled a glass with water, downing it quickly in several gulps.

"I've got a bunch of interviews lined up this morning." Amy buttered her toast, holding the knife with long, delicate fingers. "I couldn't get 'hold of the mushroom expert, so I'm going to the mushroom farm to see if I can find him. And then I'm meeting with a nurse who knows some of the people who got sick in the forest. I'm hoping to get names of people who will be willing to talk—"

"You keep saying *I*. I thought we were supposed to search for Maria together."

Amy frowned. "No. I offered to let you listen to Maria's recordings. I never said anything about teaming up. I'm here for work."

Lori poured herself a cup of coffee. She vaguely recalled inviting Amy to stay at the house but couldn't remember much else, thanks to overindulging the night before. Drinking made her anxiety worse, and that old, familiar unsettled feeling was threatening to overwhelm her.

Had she just assumed Amy'd also agreed they'd work together? It wouldn't be the first time she'd added two and two and come up with five. Like she shouldn't have assumed Julian was interested in resuming a relationship just because she was lonely and longing for their daughter.

Lori leaned against the counter, unmoored. "Then what should I do?"

She'd come to Mendocino without a plan, and this morning—after all the wine—she'd lost her way. And her resolve. Lori was a commercial realtor, not a detective, not a reporter experienced in digging for information.

Amy stared at her for a long time. Her large eyes gave her the appearance of a curious and judgmental grasshopper. She hesitated, opening and closing her mouth before finally frowning. "I don't know what you should do. What do you want to do?"

"I'm not sure," Lori replied, her voice barely above a whisper. "I want to find my daughter."

Her knees felt wobbly, and her face seemed to be tingling. Was it just the hangover, or was she on the verge of another panic attack?

Amy looked out the window into the garden. The morning fog had yet to clear. When she turned to Lori, she

92

smiled faintly. "You hit it hard last night, if you don't mind me saying. I think you should go back to bed and sleep it off." She paused, her eyes narrowing. "How about this? I'll go off and do my thing, and if I find out anything interesting, I'll let you know...and maybe you can help?"

The plan sounded vague and half-hearted, but she was out of options. Lori nodded, breathing through her nose. "Okay, then. Thank you."

Amy's grasshopper eyes softened. "Hangovers suck." She snatched her tote bag from the counter and strode to the front door, grabbing her coat from the closet in the entryway.

Lori wondered if the reporter was always this eager to work on a story, or if Amy knew more than she had let on. Then the thought was gone, and Lori was left alone in the quiet house. As she crawled back into bed, she couldn't shake the deep unease coiling in her gut like a restless serpent.

Debra Castaneda

Chapter 19

Instead of driving to the mushroom farm, Amy went to Nils Forest to see it for herself and parked in the eastern parking lot. Fog swirled around the trunks of the tall trees. On this dreary day, the forest looked downright foreboding. She had no intention of going in. No, thank you. Not after what she'd heard on the new audio files on Maria's recorder.

Because that was some crazy shit.

Amy should have gone to the police station and handed it over, but she couldn't bring herself to do it. Partly because she was sure they would dismiss her, and Amy couldn't blame them. Maria Hart had done something no sensible person would do.

As a result, she was somewhere in the forest. Dead. The victim of her own bad choices.

Amy was also sure the investigators wouldn't bother to interview the mushroom expert again, even though Maria's recordings had revealed important new information.

The parking lot was covered by a thick canopy of trees under a hazy sky. Another dreary day in Mendocino. Maria had called Nils Forest beautiful. Breathtaking. And Amy supposed it was, but she was getting "Hansel and Gretel" vibes, and nothing could compel her to enter the woods alone. Maybe she could convince Joe from the market to come with her, though he didn't seem like much of a hiker.

Which left Lori and Julian. They knew the forest. Julian worked on a ranch, and he looked the outdoorsy type, sturdy and strong. And besides, they were motivated to find their daughter. Dead or alive.

Amy's motivation was not as straightforward. She couldn't shake the feeling Maria was pulling a fast one. That she was alive somewhere, biding her time. There had always been something a little off about Maria. She was too nice, sometimes sickeningly so.

Amy was planning to look for a body, but if she found Maria alive, that would be a story—a very *big* story that could lead to very big things. Best not to examine her motivations too closely. She needed to trust her instincts as a journalist, which meant keeping Maria's last audio recordings to herself.

Three trucks rumbled into the parking lot. Moments later, a half-dozen people emerged, dressed for hiking. They quickly put on backpacks and gathered at the trailhead. No one seemed to notice her.

Amy hopped out of the car and jogged toward them. When she stopped, she was winded from the short burst of activity. Jesus. She needed to start working out or something. The group turned and eyed her with guarded expressions.

"Hi! Are you guys going out to look for Karl Ackerman?"

They shared a silent look, then one person broke away from the group—a woman of about forty, with thick dark hair styled in a severe bob and micro bangs. "We are. Can I help you?"

Amy retrieved her business card from her coat pocket and handed it to the woman. "I don't want to hold you up or anything, but I'd like to ask a few questions." When the woman began to shake her head, Amy quickly added, "I'll be quick. I promise."

The woman scratched her nose. It was covered in freckles. "It's not that. We were told not to talk to reporters."

Amy sniffed. "Really? Why not?"

"We're not authorized. The ranger is the one you want to talk to. Besides, we don't know much. We're just here to help, down from Redding. They've got people coming from all over."

A man stepped aside. "You're Amy Matthews, right? I'm local, actually. A volunteer taking them in. I'll talk to you if we make it quick."

The woman with the bob scowled. "I don't think that's a good idea, Mark."

Mark shrugged. "I listen to her all the time. She's on my favorite radio station. It's cool."

"Whatever happens is on you," the woman snapped and turned away.

Amy motioned for him to follow her, leading him toward her car and away from the rest of the group. A chill breeze swept across the hills, causing the treetops to sway and rustle. Her jacket was no match for the biting, damp weather. Mark was short, barrel-chested, with a small tight mouth and narrow green eyes. He glanced over his shoulder, then turned to her with an expectant smile.

"If you're showing them around, you must be familiar with the forest, right?" she began.

"That's right. I've been hiking Nils forever, but there are still parts that I haven't reached yet, to be completely honest. Mostly, I stick to the trails. Most people do, unless you want to get lost."

"Are you focusing on any specific locations, then?"

Mark scratched his nose. "What do you call it if I talk to you without you giving my name?"

"Off the record."

"That's it. Off the record. Can we do that?"

"Sure." Amy's heart beat a little faster. She hoped he wasn't fucking with her.

"I think I'm okay in saying no one has any idea where Karl Ackerman went. There are some lime kilns way out in the middle of the forest that take forever to get to, so it's possible he ended up there if he was looking for shelter. But the trouble is, no one's been able to get to the kilns because, for some unknown reason, people keep getting sick and have to turn back. Me included."

Amy tried to conceal her excitement. "I heard about that. Like, what kind of sick? Did you go see a doctor? What did they say?"

"It's hard to describe. Lightheaded, like I couldn't think straight. And later, I had a hard time remembering what happened, just that I was tired and nauseous for hours. Like I was getting over norovirus or something, except without the runs."

His cheeks turned red.

"Excuse my language. I would have assumed I was just coming down with something, but other people got it too. And then I got a really bad headache, so I thought maybe I'd been exposed to fumes, but that didn't make any sense. I went to emergency, and they did some blood tests, but they couldn't find anything wrong. I'm just keeping my fingers crossed whatever caused all that has disappeared."

"Off the record, does the ranger have any idea what's causing it, even if he's not ready to talk about it yet?"

"Not that I've heard, but I'll tell you something. It's weird enough to make me think there's something going on in there that we can't understand..." His voice trailed off.

"Like UFOs?"

Mark shrugged. "Maybe. Or maybe a secret government experiment that got out of hand. Or someone buried some chemicals in the dirt, and they're seeping out. Fuck if I know. I asked the ranger if he'd give us respirators, and he just about shit his pants. By the way he acts, he thinks we're hysterical or exaggerating or something. But I don't think that's an unreasonable request, considering."

"Can you call me? After you're done? Tell me what happened, off the record?"

He nodded. "Yeah, sure. I just hope I don't get sick again and have to miss work. My boss is not going to be so happy about that."

"What kind of work do you do?" Amy asked, curious. Mendocino seemed so remote. What did anybody who lived here do for a living?

"I'm a facility supervisor at a mushroom farm." He gave a sheepish grin. "This is where you say, 'A mushroom farm!' Most people do. But where do they think mushrooms come from?"

Amy's eyes widened. "You wouldn't happen to know a Gabriele Bruno, would you?"

"Yeah. I do. He's my boss. He owns the farm."

Amy couldn't believe her luck. "I'd like to talk to him for a story I'm working on. Would you mind giving me his contact info?"

When that was done and they'd exchanged numbers, Mark jogged back to the group, and Amy retreated to her car. She needed to listen to those hidden files one more time.

Amy took Maria's audio recorder out of her tote.

Chapter 20

The wind picked up and gently rocked Amy's car. She slid the headphones over her ears, leaned her head against the headrest, and pressed play.

Reality faded away while Maria talked. The recorder might have been a dinky, unreliable piece of equipment, but the audio quality was crisp and clear.

"Something amazing happened.

Gabriele Bruno is the most amazing and interesting man I've ever met. He's brilliant. We met for a drink and just talked and talked.

He said he'd never seen mycelium spread so fast before, and he was so excited about the mushroom I'd found. He's sure it's a new species of hallucinogenic mushroom. He asked me if I'd ever tried them, and I said no. And then we went to his house, and we were making out, and I told him I wanted to try mushrooms. I mean, what safer way to do it because he's an expert and knows the doses.

So I did, and it was incredible, beautiful. I felt the beauty of the world and the goodness of its people, and I just had this amazing appreciation for it all. And then I heard this voice. Maybe not an actual voice. More like a feeling. And it was telling me, begging me, to taste the mushroom I found in the forest, but I knew that Gabriele would never let me because he hadn't tested it yet.

Maybe I wasn't thinking straight, but I couldn't help myself. When Gabriele went to the bathroom, I went into his office and found it.

'Just a little,' the voice said.

I ate more than half of it by the time Gabriele found me, and he was so upset. He kept asking me how I was feeling. I could barely hear him, and I could tell he was worried but excited too.

I couldn't talk by then because the room had disappeared and I was staring up at the night sky. No stars or anything. Just blackness. And then a big zipper appeared, and when it opened, I saw a giant face staring down at me. And when it spoke, its voice was commanding but gentle.

'Go into the forest,' it said. 'You are no longer alone. You belong to me. For I am the seasons and the rebirth.'

The skin of the giant in the sky began to pucker and bubble until it slipped off. And then I was crying. Reaching up for it. But it disappeared into the darkness, and I was alone.

When I woke up, it was morning. Gabriele asked me to explain what I'd experienced, and I lied. Said I couldn't remember because I didn't want him to tell me it was just a wild trip. It wasn't. It was real, and I knew what I had to do next. Go into Nils Forest and find more of those mushrooms."

The recording ended. Amy also knew what *she* had to do next.

She started the car. "Stupid bitch," Amy muttered, throwing it into reverse.

Chapter 21

The doorbell chimed loudly, interrupting David's shower. For the first time in months, he was bathing without the indignity of the plastic chair.

Whoever was outside began banging on the front door.

Cursing, David toweled off and quickly dressed, his hands and feet cooperating so easily, he hardly gave the process any thought except for a moment of wonder. He threw the door open, revealing a stranger on the other side. Handsome, with a profusion of windswept dark hair.

"Yes?" David barked out.

The man looked past him, into the house. "I heard you were having some issues with fungus."

With one hand on the door, ready to shut it in the man's face, David asked, "Who told you that?"

The man grinned sheepishly. "I'm afraid I forgot to write it down. But someone called me. Asked me to take a look. I'm an expert on fungus and mold. I don't normally do inspections, but I can probably point you in the right direction to help you solve the problem."

"Is that right?" David said.

The man tilted his head to the side, a mischievous glint in his eyes. "Wouldn't you like to know more about them? Because I can tell you. I can tell you everything you want to know."

The man's voice sent David's heart thumping. There was something off about this visitor.

"Who are you?"

"Gabriele Bruno. I'm a mycologist. I own Bruno's Mushroom Farm and teach at the local college." He paused. "We know someone in common. Maria. Maria Hart?"

A shudder of cold swept through David. "You said *know*. She's been gone for six months. Do you know something about her? Is she still alive?"

"That I cannot say," Gabriele replied, voice tinged with regret. "May I come in? It's a bit cold out here."

David stepped aside. Gabriele's gaze swept across the living room.

When David had awoken the morning after the tendrils engulfed him, the thick fibrous mat in the living room had vanished, with only a narrow white trail linking the front door to the mushrooms growing behind his headboard.

Gabriele's eyes landed on the white threads along the floor molding. "Interesting," he said, as if the sight did not surprise him at all.

"What is it?" David asked.

Without taking his eyes from the trail, Gabriele said, "Mycelium. Your question is also interesting. You want to know what it is, not how to get rid of it."

David remembered something, and the hair on the back of his neck lifted. "Maria said she was going to meet a mushroom expert the last time we spoke." His voice rose. "Was that you?"

Gabriele had moved to the wall, inspecting it through squinted eyes, hands behind his back. Ignoring David's question, Gabriele turned to face him, eyebrows knitting together. "How are you feeling, Mr. Eager? I've heard that you haven't been yourself for quite some time now, but you appear to be in good health." He gave a sidelong glance to the trail of mycelium leading to the hallway. "It's interesting, isn't it?"

"How did you know?" David stammered.

Gabriele stepped closer and patted his arm. "We can talk about that later. I'm here, really, to make sure that your fungal ambassadors are where they should be—out of sight, far from prying eyes. You'll want to make sure your cleaning lady doesn't go into your bedroom and disturb them. They're important, you know. To your continued health. The mycelium is here to make a few more important deposits, a little more powerful now that we know you're tolerating it so well."

David's mouth opened, then closed.

The growth of mushrooms in his bedroom evidently had something to do with his recovery, and this stranger seemed to know all about it. But how? Was it another hallucination? Was his recovery all in his head? Would he snap back to reality, finding himself on the floor, crawling toward his bed, screaming for help?

Gabriele seemed to register his confusion. "I know it's a lot to process, David. That's why I'm here. In a few days, I think you'll be well enough to take a walk with me into the forest. See what there is to see. Would you like that?"

David's head spun, and he nodded, relief washing over him.

Gabrielle turned to the kitchen. "Mind if I get some water?"

"Go ahead." The words came croaking out.

A few moments later, Gabriele came back and handed David a tall glass brimming with water, then searched through his pockets until he found what he was looking for. With a charming, lopsided smile, he pulled out a small paper bag, opened it, and held it out for inspection.

David peered inside. There was something at the bottom. Dried, shriveled, and nearly black.

"I brought this for you," Gabriele said. "It should help speed things along."

David gazed at the bag for what felt like an eternity, but Gabriele didn't seem to mind. He sank into the nearest chair and, in one fluid, elegant movement, crossed his legs. The paper bag remained on his lap. David looked away, biting the inside of his cheek so hard the metallic taste of blood bloomed in his mouth.

"You're going to be fine." Gabriele had a rich, melodious voice. Reassuring. Soothing.

David swallowed. "How fine?"

Gabriele held out the open bag. "*Very* fine."

David stretched out his hand. It didn't shake in the slightest.

Chapter 22

At Bruno's Mushroom Farm, an employee told Amy that Gabriele Bruno was out for the morning.

So, Amy moved on to her next interview—the one with the nurse who had looked after some of the sick rescuers. He simply repeated what he had already told her over the phone. But when they were done, he gave her the name of one of the sickened hikers, a friend who owned a kayak and bike business.

Amy drove to the shop and introduced herself. The owner had a white beard that would make Santa Claus envious, and he was happy to talk. After taking his information—his name was Ian—she asked what he thought was going on in the forest.

"I don't know. But some people like a little drama, and they'll find it one way or another."

She smiled. "You may be right, but I've heard some interesting theories since I got here. Including one about UFOs."

"I heard that one too. It's laughable. In Mendocino? I don't think so. You know, the only thing I can think of has to do with some old lime kilns in the forest. There used to be a rail line to transport that stuff. It's all covered up now, but maybe whatever chemicals they used back then are still around and are making people sick along the old railbed. Have you looked into that?"

Amy shook her head. "No. But I will. Have you been out to the kilns?"

Ian stroked his beard. "Not for a lot of years. My hikes only go in a couple of miles these days."

"Do you know anybody who's been to the kilns?" she pressed.

He nodded. "As it happens, I do. I've got a buddy who's been out there."

"Would you mind giving me his name?"

"I don't see why not," Ian replied easily. "His name is Julian Cruz. He owns a bison farm outside of town. It's easy enough to find."

Amy sighed. Julian and Lori had said they knew the forest well, but they hadn't struck her as hikers. She had hoped to find someone to take her into Nils Forest, and now it seemed like Maria's parents were the most logical choice.

Her next stop was the ranger station. She'd called the assignment desk and asked them to arrange the interview, knowing it would be harder for the ranger to say no to her editor.

She drove the winding roads to the Nils Forest Ranger Station. Her phone rang—Mark from the search team. They'd made it about an hour into their hike when a couple of them began to get sick, so they turned around.

Good timing. More for her to discuss with the ranger.

It was a long drive to the far north end of the park. Towering redwoods surrounded the wood-shingled building with green-painted window frames. Isolated, but not a bad place to work.

Amy found Doyle Bronson inside, sitting behind an ancient metal desk, hunched over a stack of papers. He glanced up and gave her a curt nod, telling her everything she needed to know. Bronson did *not* want to talk with her, and he intended to keep his responses short and vague.

"Mr. Bronson!" She greeted him in an overly cheerful tone. "Thank you for taking the time to meet with me. I'm so glad you were available on such short notice. My editor is chomping at the bit for this story, and I'm hoping to get it to the station as soon as possible."

Bronson raised a hand. "I'm a little confused about what story you're working on, Miss Matthews. We already released a statement to all media outlets, yours included. And at this time, there are no new developments to report."

"My story is about Nils Forest," Amy replied.

He didn't offer her a seat, so she took the wooden chair opposite his desk, pulled out her audio recorder, attached the microphone, and pressed the red record button. Amy leaned forward and positioned the mic a few inches below his chin.

"Can you please count to ten while I check the audio levels?"

"But—"

"Don't worry. This will only take a few minutes."

Despite his smooth and plump face, the ranger's age showed in the deep rings around his neck. He had thinning yellow hair, a narrow mustache, and blue eyes behind wire-rimmed glasses. Bronson exhaled loudly, resigning himself to the interview, despite his better judgment.

Amy would have to go in quickly and aggressively and hope to catch him off guard. "Have you heard about the rumors spreading online? About the forest?"

Bronson leaned forward and placed his arms on the desk, snorting dismissively. "Unfortunately. They're ridiculous and only serve as a distraction."

Amy shrugged, determined to break through his resistance. "Ridiculous or not, the internet has a way of blowing up even the craziest stories. And as they say, where there's smoke, there's fire. I spoke with a nurse at the hospital who confirmed they've treated several people who got sick in the forest. He said they don't know what made those people sick. My own sources say your search team from Redding had to turn back this morning after getting sick, abandoning their search for Karl Ackerman. What's your take on that?"

"I hadn't heard. I'm sure there will be toxicology reports," Bronson replied stiffly.

"I'm told that blood tests from the last group were negative or inconclusive. That's strange, isn't it?"

"I don't know," Bronson said. "I'm not a medical expert."

Amy's butt was starting to go numb from the hard chair. "I've also heard that some of the search teams have asked for respirators."

A flicker of unease passed over Bronson's face. "We don't have that kind of equipment. There's no need."

"Have any search teams made it as far as the kilns?"

Bronson refused to meet her eyes. "Not recently."

"When was the last time anyone has done a thorough search of the kilns?"

Bronson stared out the window, stalling. "I believe it was after Maria Hart went missing."

Amy nearly dropped her microphone. "But that was six months ago. Are you saying that people have been getting sick since then?

Bronson's gaze remained fixed on the trees in the distance. "Yes."

"Have you alerted anyone? Aren't there officials who should know about this?"

"I have submitted my reports," Bronson retorted.

Ignoring his irritation, Amy continued. "So, in the absence of any solid information about what's causing people to get sick in the forest, it's not really any surprise that the public will come up with their own theories, and that's why rumors are blowing up online."

"I can't help what people say online." Bronson pressed his lips together as if vowing not to say any more.

Amy knew she had stumbled onto a big story. She just couldn't understand why it hadn't made the national news yet. The ranger had publicly stated they'd searched the forest and found nothing, but he conveniently failed to mention they had left out a large portion of it.

Bronson straightened. "Are we finished here?"

Amy took a moment to consider her options. Bronson wasn't likely to give any newsworthy quotes while she was recording, but his evasions and "no comments" would speak volumes. She decided on a different approach.

Amy put the mic on the desk and clicked the red button on the recorder. "It's off now."

She looked Bronson in the eye.

"I think you already know this, but you sound like you're trying to hide something. If I play any of this interview in my story, it's not going to look very good. So how about I leave the recorder off and you tell me, off the record, what's going on?"

Bronson's smooth face tightened, eyes darting to the door as if contemplating his escape. He gave a sharp nod.

Amy cleared her throat. "Do you think it's possible the missing people ended up at the kilns and maybe something happened to them there?"

Bronson shook his head. "It's not the kind of place you stumble upon by accident. It's deep in the forest and difficult to reach. I can't emphasize that enough."

"But I've seen pictures of the kilns. They look incredible. Maybe the missing people saw pictures too but didn't understand how hard it is to get there?"

"Even if they had tried to make the trek, there's no guarantee they would have made it. Most people give up after a third of the way. None of the individuals who've disappeared were experienced hikers. They weren't equipped for a long hike."

"What if they were attacked and taken to the kilns?"

Bronson snorted. "Unless the attacker was as strong as Bigfoot, that's unlikely."

"Bigfoot is one of the online theories," Amy said dryly. "What do you think is happening? What's keeping your people from getting there?"

The ranger's eyebrows lifted. "I don't know. All I know for certain is that it's definitely not UFOs or any of the other crackpot theories floating around."

Amy bit her lip and considered her next move, concluding she had to push him even harder. "I've heard that after the big windstorm a while back, the one that did so much damage, mushrooms helped the forest to regenerate. Do you think there's any connection there? Between what's happening now and the mushrooms?"

Bronson rolled his eyes. "Miss Matthews, this is Northern California. There are mushrooms everywhere, and Nils Forest is full of them. Always has been. Mushrooms are an important part of the ecosystem here. People come from all over to forage for them. The community college teaches classes on mushroom identification and cooking with mushrooms, and they lead groups into the forest for mushroom hunts. There's even an annual mushroom festival. The Fungus Fair. So, no, I do not believe there is any connection between mushrooms and our teams getting sick. Who, by the way, did not eat them or tamper with them. We're not the morons you seem to think we are because we did determine that. So, what connection could there possibly be?"

Amy knew the answer to that question lay with Gabriele Bruno, the man Maria Hart had spent the night with before she vanished. She grabbed her audio equipment, thanked Bronson for his time, and quickly made her exit.

Chapter 23

For the second time, Amy pulled into the parking lot of Bruno's Mushroom Farm. This was no small side hustle. The full-scale operation spanned several acres of land dotted with weathered wooden structures. She presumed that's where they grew the mushrooms. There were a few smaller buildings made of corrugated metal painted in bright colors. Towering redwood trees lined the edges of the property.

Amy stepped out of her car and followed the path toward the office, gravel crunching underfoot. She went into the plain, single-room building. A woman was on the phone, apparently engrossed in a heated conversation with a supplier.

"Hold on a moment," the woman said into the receiver, staring at Amy.

"I have an appointment with Gabriele Bruno," Amy lied.

"Go back outside and make a left. He's around the corner." The woman returned to her conversation.

At the end of the path, Amy came to a sudden stop. Gabriele Bruno's office was in an old shipping container boldly painted a bright red. She pushed open the door and stepped inside.

It wasn't at all what she expected—warm wooden planks covered the interior, with a long farm table against one wall and a chandelier made of metal mesh and twinkling lights. It was dreamy and magical.

Amy was too busy taking it all in to notice the small alcove at the back or the dark curtain concealing it.

A man stepped out. "Can I help you?"

Amy stared. The man standing in front of her must be Gabriele Bruno. For one thing, he looked like a Gabriele. For another, it was no wonder Maria had been attracted to him—"handsome" didn't even begin to describe his looks.

She cleared her throat and introduced herself. As soon as he heard she'd known Maria, his demeanor changed. He became stiff and guarded.

"And you work at the same radio station she did?" Gabriele asked, frowning.

"That's right. In fact, I took the job she vacated when she didn't come back." Amy had chosen her words carefully and was pleased they seemed to have the desired effect.

"Didn't come back," he echoed, his frown deepening. "You make it sound like it was her choice."

Amy's hands and feet tingled. This was getting interesting. "Maybe it was. No one's been able to find her. Or a body. I do have some questions I'd like to ask you about Mar—"

"I've already told what little I know to the police."

"I'm sure you have," she replied mildly, gesturing at the table. "Mind if I sit? Take some notes?" No need to take out the audio equipment. It would just make the man nervous, and she didn't need a sound bite from him. Yet.

He glanced over his shoulder at whatever was behind the curtain, as if he couldn't wait to return, and pinched the bridge of his aquiline nose. "Of course, please. I'm sorry. I wasn't expecting any visitors today."

Gabriele settled himself into the opposite chair, eyeing her with barely disguised trepidation that would have been puzzling if she hadn't listened to Maria's audio recordings.

"Besides owning this farm," she began, "I understand that you're a mushroom expert—"

"A mycologist," Gabriele interrupted. "Yes. I have a Ph.D. in mycology and plant microbiology."

Amy dutifully jotted the information down in her reporter's notebook. "I imagine you've heard about all the people getting sick in Nils Forest?"

"Yes? But I—" Gabriele's dark eyes clouded.

It was Amy's turn to interrupt. "I have just one question. Do you think it's possible mushrooms or a fungus of some sort might be responsible for making them sick?"

An odd noise, like a croak, escaped Gabriele's throat. "I can't imagine how. Some of the symptoms are consistent with toxic mushrooms, but no one ate any, as far as I know."

Luckily, Amy'd had time to consider this during the drive. She didn't know much about mushrooms, aside from enjoying them cooked in butter and garlic. But she did recall a scene from a movie she'd watched as a child. "What about their spores? Is that what they're called? Spores? That's how mushrooms spread, right? Could those get into the air and make people sick?"

Gabriele froze, his gaze shifting inward. Then he seemed to remember she was still there, waiting for a response, and he shook his head. "Yes, that's what spores do, but for them to make people sick, that way and so quickly, that would be unprecedented."

"Okay. But is it possible?"

Gabriele's eyes narrowed. "In the movies, but not in real life. Is this really what you wanted to talk about?" His tone oozed contempt.

"That's not my only question. Like I said, I was friends with Maria, so I'm just curious. Did you sleep with her?"

Gabriele's mouth fell open. When he closed it, his face had reddened. "I'd just met her." He managed to sound sufficiently scandalized.

117

Amy snorted. "Oh, like that's ever stopped anyone." Especially someone as hot as Gabriele Bruno. He probably couldn't buy toilet paper without getting hit on.

"I don't see how that's any of your business, in your capacity as a reporter."

"We were friends. She might have said a thing or two." She wiggled her eyebrows suggestively.

Gabriele tugged on his bottom lip. "You spoke to her? After we met in Mendocino?"

"Mm, that's a little complicated," she admitted. "So, did you guys hook up, or what? Or, to put it another way, did you tell the police you two got together that night, after she was supposed to have gone missing in the forest?"

The color drained from his face. "How...?"

"That, I'm afraid, I can't tell you. I think you spent more time with Maria than you said. But I might be willing to keep that to myself if you tell me when, exactly, was the last time you saw her alive and well?"

Gabriele rubbed his chin. "Not since that night, when we were together."

"What about in the morning?"

"She left without saying goodbye." He gave a little shrug, as if having women tiptoe out of his bedroom was a frequent occurrence.

"And you haven't seen her since?"

Gabriele shook his head so hard a curl of brown hair fell in front of his forehead. "No! I would have told the police."

Would he have? Amy held the thought and went in for the last question. "I keep hearing about the lime kilns in the middle of Nils Forest. Ever been there?"

Gabriele swiped away the stray curl. "No. I like a good hike, but that's too far for me."

Amy quickly wrapped up the interview. As she prepared to leave, Gabriele became much friendlier, nearly giddy. He even walked her to her car. If he was concerned about how Amy knew he had spent the night with Maria, he didn't show it.

She drove away, stealing a quick glance in the rearview mirror. Gabriele was still standing there, legs spread wide, hands clasped behind his neck.

"Liar," she muttered.

Debra Castaneda

Chapter 24

Lori had just come back from a run along the headlands when Amy arrived, Julian on her heels. She noticed them exchanging a quick glance when they entered the kitchen and knew something was up. Lori downed a glass of water and two more ibuprofen to chase away the lingering headache. Julian sat at the table, his posture rigid, lips pressed tightly together.

"Does someone want to tell me what's going on?" Lori asked. There was a quiver in her voice. Had Maria's body been discovered?

Julian pressed the heel of his palm into his forehead but remained silent.

Amy sighed and dropped her tote bag on the table with a thud. "You know those recordings Maria made? There were more of them."

"I don't understand," Lori said.

Julian looked up at her, a muscle in his jaw twitching. "Remember when I was fumbling around with Maria's recorder? I pushed some buttons by mistake. But whatever I did revealed some tracks that were hidden or something. More of Maria's audio diary. Amy's heard them, and I think we should too."

"But you should prepare yourselves." Amy's tone was somber.

Suddenly lightheaded, Lori leaned against the counter. "Prepare ourselves for what?" Her ears began to ring.

Amy collapsed into a chair. "To hear Maria talking about some pretty weird stuff."

She dug into her bag and pulled out a recorder. Not the small, fragile silver one from yesterday, but a larger, bulkier piece of equipment.

"I figured out a way to transfer Maria's files to my machine so we can listen to it on the speaker. Are you ready, or do you want a little extra time?"

"Now," Lori and Julian said in unison.

"All right." Amy pushed the play button.

Forest sounds filled the kitchen, wind in the trees and the sounds of birds. Maria's voice describing her encounter with Gabriele Bruno, hearing about the Aztecs worshiping psychedelic mushrooms, then eating one herself. When her story was done, the audio ended abruptly.

Julian shifted in his chair. "Who is this Bruno guy?"

"Gabriele Bruno. He's a mushroom expert. He has a Ph.D. in mycology. I talked to him this morning, and I'm convinced he knows more than he's saying. But I don't think he took advantage of Maria."

Amy paused, as though carefully considering her next words.

"I don't mean to sound harsh, but I know Maria better than both of you, and I know how charming and persuasive she can be. And single-minded. Things don't happen *to* her. She *makes* them happen."

A part of Lori wanted to run to her bedroom and hide, shutting the door behind her. She knew Amy meant well, but hearing Maria's voice was painful, and not knowing what had happened to her was terrifying.

Julian also seemed uneasy, his gaze fixed on the recorder as if it might sprout teeth and bite him. He extended his arm to her, catching Lori by surprise. She walked over and grasped it, taking the seat next to him. Julian clutched her hand with strong, brown fingers. A distant memory slipped into her consciousness—a hike years ago in Nils Forest, climbing hills together, Julian in the lead, pulling her up a steep slope. Lori scooted her chair closer to his, and his arm came around her shoulder.

"Okay, here's the next file." Amy hit play.

Maria's voice continued, but the forest sounds were gone, replaced by the hollowness of a cave or stone building. Her voice echoed off the walls while she spoke.

"I walked for hours, so many hours, into the forest. I was lost, but I did not feel lost. I had guides: the birds, a squirrel. When it got dark, glowing mushrooms lit the way. And then I was there. The place where I was called to be. There was a fire burning inside the stone building, and I saw that I wasn't alone. There were people there. They said they'd been waiting, and when I asked if they were waiting for me, they said they didn't know because I hadn't been tested yet.

They called the place The Kilns and showed me the same kind of mushroom I had taken, the one I had picked in the forest."

Maria again described experiencing visions of a god in the sky, wearing a cloak of skin, and hearing a voice from the clouds.

"The people in the woods said the sky had opened up to them too, and they also heard a voice. They said they'd been waiting ever since."

She said the god needed a sacrifice, so she sliced her arm and bled before cutting the arms of the others. Maria began referring to the others in the kilns as "her people," and she described how she could command mushrooms to defend the camp.

Lori glanced at Julian several times, stunned by Maria's story but not knowing what to make of it. He returned her gaze without expression.

But when Maria again mentioned Gabriele Bruno, they both stared at the recorder intently.

"*Gabriele came the next day. I sent a few of the strongest men to help him bring supplies so we can stay in the kilns and prepare.*

And now, the spores are keeping the others away so we won't be bothered anymore.

Oh shit. People are coming. How…no, no, no."

The recording ended abruptly.

Chapter 25

A sharp taste rose in the back of Lori's throat, and a tremor passed through her body. She blamed herself for whatever had happened to Maria.

Her daughter had never truly understood how much she was loved and wanted, that Lori had regretted giving her up. And now, Maria's emotional scar had transformed into…what?

"She…Why…?" she managed to say before tears choked off the words.

Julian massaged his forehead, his gaze still fixed on the recorder. Gradually, he shifted his attention toward her.

"Lor? Are you all right?"

"No!" she cried. "I'm *not* all right. Our daughter had a full-on mental breakdown in the middle of the forest and…"

Julian suddenly seemed to notice Amy staring at them. He jumped to his feet, grabbed Lori by the arm, and led her through the back door into the garden.

He glanced at Amy over his shoulder. "Stay here."

Amy shrugged.

Lori didn't resist Julian guiding her toward the gate, one arm around her waist. They stepped onto the headlands, the vast sea crashing against the cliffs below. The cold wind clawed at their faces, but Lori was too lost in her own thoughts to notice.

"You need to calm down so we can talk this through."

Always the practical one.

Lori raked a hand through her hair. "What's there to talk through? You heard her! She sounded like a raving lunatic, and it's all because of me. *I* did this to her. Her own mother abandoned her, and now she's...unstable because how else could she believe such outrageous things?"

Julian's fingers spasmed at her waist. "She's under the influence of hallucinogens, Lori. Magic mushrooms." He paused, then turned and looked her in the eye. "How much did you tell Maria about my grandfather?"

The question forced Lori to focus. She took a deep breath and wiped her eyes with the backs of her hands. Lori reflected, trying to recall exactly what she'd shared with Maria. "I told her as much as I could remember. That he was famous in his village in Mexico and that people came from all over to see him. That he was a brujo, from a long line of brujos. And that you used to laugh about it. You used to say you wished you'd inherited his skills because you could have set up a side business in high school."

Julian's eyebrows furrowed. "And how did Maria act when you told her?"

"Excited. Frustrated because I couldn't answer all her questions." She looked out over the gray-green water. "That's when she lost interest in me, I could tell. I was just the boring white lady who abandoned her, and you were the dark, handsome, interesting guy with a fairy tale history."

"Hardly." Julian snorted, and they walked slowly down the path. "But it still doesn't make sense. She's obviously smart. Amy said she got a job at the radio station straight out of college, and that's pretty rare. She studied journalism and knows how to do her research. That's probably what she did when you told her about me and my grandfather. You heard those recordings. She found some hallucinogenic mushrooms, and the mushroom expert talked about Aztec shamans using them in their rituals. And then guess what happens? She takes them and has an experience. It was in her head all along. Practically preordained."

They finally arrived at the cliff's edge. The cry of seagulls overhead competed with the constant rumble of the restless ocean. Lori watched the waves crash against a rock arch. As the tide receded, the waves caressed the small beach of pebbles with a hissing sound. It calmed her nerves, but only slightly.

"What are we going to do?"

Julian let out a deep sigh. "We need to talk to Amy."

The tall, bird-like girl had brewed a pot of coffee and set out shortbread cookies. What Lori really wanted, and badly, was a drink. But when she went to the refrigerator for a bottle of chardonnay, Amy slammed the door shut.

"That's not a good idea with what I'm thinking," she explained.

Lori picked up a cookie. "And that would be what?"

"You're going to think it's crazy." Amy regarded them anxiously, pacing the length of the room.

Lori shrugged. It couldn't be any crazier than everything else that was happening.

"The only way you're ever going to get closure on this is for you to find her. Or, I'm sorry to say it, find her body." Amy put her palms on the table. "If we tell the police about the recording, they'll just write her off even more. They'll for sure think she's dead, and they'll say, 'Gee, thank you. Case closed.' Maybe they'll try again with the search parties, and we all know how that's going to turn out."

Lori stared at the table. "But what about what she said? About the spores that make people sick? Do we really believe that?"

Amy began pacing again. "The cause doesn't matter. Something is making people sick, and whatever it is, it's probably in the air. We need respirators."

Julian shifted in his chair. "They can't be *that* hard to get."

Lori studied Amy. All arms and legs, but not in a fit, athletic way. "No offense, but you don't look the outdoorsy type. We're not as young as we used to be, but I'm sure we can still make it to the kilns. But I'm not so sure you're up to it. There's a lot of vertical, and I'm guessing it's six miles to the kilns, at least."

Amy scoffed. "I'm not even thirty. How hard can it be?"

"Very hard," Julian said. "And I'm not comfortable going on a hike without letting the police know about Gabriele Bruno. What if he's got Maria under his control? What if she's his prisoner in the forest?"

Lori turned to Julian in surprise. "As much as I'm worried about Maria, she didn't sound like a prisoner to me."

"But this Bruno guy is into mushrooms, right?" Julian spread his hands wide. "He probably knows what he's doing. You said she's vulnerable."

"She is." Lori turned to Julian. "Maybe you should go see him. Tell him you're her father and see what you can get out of him."

"We need to stay away from Gabriele," Amy said firmly. "I already freaked him out enough, and you heard what Maria said. He was helping her. We just need to get to the kilns ourselves."

"And then what?" Julian asked.

"And then we'll know more than we do now."

Amy's cell phone chimed. She listened to whoever was on the other end, and her eyes narrowed. Amy ended the call and put her phone on the table.

"This is bad," she said.

Every worst-case scenario played out in Lori's head.

Julian set down his mug, coffee sloshing over the rim. "What?"

Amy's eyes flitted between them. "You remember Joe, right? The guy who works at the market? He says some kid came out of the forest and he's telling crazy stories."

Chapter 26

The winding road led to a mobile home park sandwiched between a grove of towering redwood trees and a creek. It was a beautiful place, but the beauty stopped at the park's entrance. Amy soon found herself driving along a desolate dirt pathway devoid of greenery and filled with sad attempts to brighten up the place: rusted signs with homey welcomes, faded pink flamingos, and rows of plastic flowers caked with dirt.

She pulled her car into a space next to a blue trailer, a rainbow fish flag fluttering in the wind. The air smelled of salt and sea.

Amy took a deep breath. As much as her assignment editor annoyed her, he always had her safety in mind. But now she was on her own, pursuing an interview with a total stranger in a remote location. She couldn't shake a sense of unease. There was something about this story making her itchy all over. What the hell was Maria up to?

She made her way up to No. 46, the metal steps creaking under her boots. A black truck loaded with fishing gear was parked outside. A dog began barking, hurling itself at the front door. No knocking required.

The screen door opened, and a pale face peered out. "Are you Amy?" His voice could hardly be heard over the dog's angry barking. He gave it a gentle shove. "Oh, come on, buddy. Calm the fuck down."

"I'm Amy Matthews." Amy stuck out her hand. "You want to put that dog in a bedroom or someplace while we talk?"

"Kyle Arnold. And this is Rufus. Don't worry, he's friendly." The young man opened the door a little wider. The dog shoved his head between Kyle's knees and looked up at Amy with hopeful eyes.

A voice called out from inside the house. "Just tell her it's your emotional support animal."

"Fuck off," Kyle shouted over his shoulder. "He loves that joke."

Kyle gestured toward a brown recliner, its arms patched with black electrical tape. The cheap wood-paneled walls were bare. No plants. No books. An enormous TV sat atop a console. The room was dreary but spotless. The sharp scent of lemon lingered in the air, as if someone had recently cleaned with disinfectant.

Kyle settled onto the fake leather couch, knees tucked to his chest, and pulled a blanket up to his chin. Amy needn't have worried about the dog. Rufus hopped on the couch and disappeared under the blanket.

Kyle looked like a model on his day off. He was doing everything he could to downplay the fact he'd won the genetic lottery. Unbrushed auburn hair, baggy clothes hiding a tall, elegant frame. There was no hiding that jawline or those cheekbones. But it appeared the guy hadn't slept in weeks. The dark circles under his eyes had a purple sheen to them.

She took out her recorder and plugged in the microphone, but Kyle reared his head back. "I don't want to talk into that thing."

Amy set the equipment on the coffee table with a sigh. "Joe told you I was a radio reporter, right? We need recorded interviews for our stories."

"I don't want anyone to recognize my voice." Kyle pressed his back against the couch.

He was breathing rapidly. If she didn't calm him down, he'd have a full-blown panic attack, and she'd lose the interview. Amy raised her hands in the air.

"Okay, okay. Not a problem. Why don't we just talk first?"

Kyle exhaled loudly. "Thank you. Thank you. And thanks for coming to see me too."

"Joe said you went to see the police?"

"I did. Right away. The cop at the desk wrote down what I said, but she thought I was high, so I don't know what she did with the information. I wasn't high, just in case you're wondering. I've been clean for more than a week. I gave them this address, but nobody ever came. I didn't know what to do, so I called Joe. And he said you'd be interested to hear what I have to say."

"I am. I'm very interested."

Amy sat expectantly, waiting for Kyle to say something. He squirmed a little and pulled the blanket up tighter but didn't say a word.

"Can you tell me about the forest? Why did you go in, and what did you find in the woods?"

Kyle inhaled slowly, releasing his breath in a long sigh. His eyes met hers.

"A couple of my friends went into the forest to hang out months ago, and they just…disappeared. I was staying in a campground by the river, and we kept hearing these rumors about people living at the kilns. And some trippy stuff, like crazy storms right over the middle of the forest. Someone said they found blood and gross shit near the kilns, but when they went back to try to find it again, it was gone, and they started feeling sick, so they had to leave."

"So what made *you* want to go into the forest?"

Kyle shrugged and looked away. "I wanted to know what happened to my friends. If they went in and stayed there, it either had to be good, or they needed help."

"Did you find them?"

He shook his head. "No. I know the forest pretty well. I got close to the kilns, but I ran into some girls before I got there. They said they were just partying and stuff, but I knew they were lying because their campsite was pretty elaborate."

"How many people were there?" Amy asked, one foot nervously twitching against the floor.

"I'm not sure because people were coming and going all the time. I saw some old people who used to hang outside the shelter, and some teenagers too. But everybody looked different. Like, better. I think there were other camps too. So I was like, well, whatever. They were really into the magic mushroom thing, and everybody was doing it with everybody, so it was cool for a while. The girls were mostly hot, and the 'shrooms were awesome. Plus, it was free, and so was the food. They had plenty of it."

Amy's mouth had gone dry. She was leaning forward now, pressing her hands into her knees. "And then what happened?"

"And then things really got fucked up." Kyle shuddered. "This girl, she was super intense. She wanted this guy named Jordan to eat a mushroom they found in front of their tent. They said he was meant to take it. But that was crazy because it might be poisonous, so he refused, and she totally flipped out. And when he told her to take it herself, she said she'd already taken the mushroom meant for her and that she'd passed the test. And that he had to pass the test too if he wanted to stay. But Jordan kept saying no, and then everybody got on his case and told him the Spore Queen would deal with him later."

Amy's foot began tapping the floor. "Who's the Spore Queen?"

"I don't know. I never got to meet her, but they said they loved her, and she was going to help them do amazing things for the planet."

"What happened to Jordan?"

"I think someone gave him something because later he was totally out of it. They took him away after that. I was pretty out of it myself, so I don't know where they went, but I think they took him to see the Spore Queen. He never came back."

Amy's pulse was racing. "What do you think happened to him?"

"I don't know for sure, but I think he may have died. Some old dude came over from another camp, and he was wearing this stuff. It looked like an animal skin, all bloody and shit, and everyone acted like it was perfectly normal. I heard someone say it was too bad Jordan hadn't passed the test. So that freaked me out, and that night, I pretended to eat the mushroom this girl gave me. But after everyone fell asleep, I was out of there."

Amy's mind reeled, trying to process Kyle's bizarre story. Tents. Nomads and runaway teenagers mysteriously transformed. A psychedelic utopia both sinister and strange. If she hadn't heard Maria's audio recordings herself, she never would have believed him.

Could Maria be the Spore Queen?

Jesus. Maria was just not that special. For all her charm, she'd worked an ordinary job with shitty hours for shitty pay. It was no surprise she'd seduced Gabriele Bruno. Maria's beauty and charisma had always drawn people in. But this was bonkers.

Amy looked at Kyle as though he knew the answers. Then she dug into her tote bag and pulled out a manila folder filled with copies of newspaper clippings and photographs. She lined them up on the coffee table.

"Do you recognize any of these people?" she asked.

Kyle rocked back and forth, Rufus whimpering in protest. "A few of them," he said in a small voice. "The girl with the long hair is Megan. That girl is Jennifer."

"Did you know they disappeared in the forest? It was big news at the time."

"No. I don't watch the news much. And Megan didn't say anything, except how amazing it was to be around her friends."

Amy blinked, slowly connecting the dots.

A cult. That's what they were dealing with. Some weird fungus cult.

With Maria as their leader? The Spore Queen? No way.

Chapter 27

If she hadn't taken a shortcut on a narrow, heavily forested road, Amy might not have noticed the car following her—an older model silver sedan so nondescript it seemed to blend in with its surroundings.

But she overshot the way into town, and when she made a U-turn, so did the silver car. And when Amy stopped at a café for a coffee and a think before heading to Lori's house, the silver car parked down the street.

She drove aimlessly around the village, and the car followed. Amy couldn't get a good look at the driver, but they were wearing a baseball cap.

The hairs on the back of her neck prickled.

Her hands shook when she pulled into the library parking lot. She grabbed her tote bag and rushed inside on shaky legs. Amy took a seat at a table facing the front door and waited. Moments later, a man wearing a baseball cap walked in, hands stuck in his pockets.

He was as generic as the car he drove. Medium height. Medium build. Pudgy face. Mud-speckled boots. Amy'd just heard about a cult hanging out in Nils Forest, and suddenly, she was being followed. The man kept his eye on her while he pretended to browse the new releases.

Whoever he was, she wasn't about to lead him back to Lori's house.

She quickly stood and hurried to the bathroom. Luckily, it was located at the end of a long hallway next to an exit. Before the stranger could follow her, she ducked outside. Instead of heading back to her car, she broke into a jog toward the headlands, glancing nervously over her shoulder the entire way.

When Amy finally arrived at the house, breathless and with a stitch in her side, Lori and Julian emerged from the bedroom on the lower level. Both were flushed and slightly disheveled. It looked like they'd found something to do while she was gone. Good for them.

She paused for a moment to catch her breath, adrenaline coursing through her veins.

"We have a problem," she said, then recounted the events with the silver car and the man with the ball cap.

Julian strode toward the entryway and peered out of the shutters.

Lori led Amy into the kitchen. "How did your interview go? What did he say?"

Amy hadn't thought that far ahead yet.

Hey, I just heard your daughter might be involved in a mushroom cult deep in the forest, and they're using drugs, and there's some dude hanging around, wearing a deer skin.

She could imagine how that would play out. They'd insist on going to the police or hiring a cult deprogrammer. Neither would get Amy into Nils Forest to find Maria.

It didn't take a genius to figure out the people who disappeared in the woods weren't really missing. They'd found a new life in the forest. But how Maria had convinced them—or forced them—to stay was a big story, and Amy was the one to break it.

And what might happen next played out like a movie in her head. Appearances on talk shows, a book deal, a documentary, even a job in Washington D.C. or New York. And money. She'd have to be able to support herself since

Maria was alive and Amy selling the San Francisco apartment was no longer possible.

So, Amy chose her words carefully.

"His name is Kyle, and he said he met a bunch of people hanging out in the forest. It's like a new-age group or something, and they're really into hallucinogenic mushrooms. I described Maria, and he said he hadn't seen her, but he was only at one camp, and there were several others." She paused. "I think she's there. In fact, I'm sure of it."

Julian jerked his head back. "But why has no one found her? After all this time? After so many searches?"

"Nobody's found *any* of these people. Because the searchers keep getting sick." Amy looked at Lori with unblinking eyes. "So if we want to find Maria, it's up to us."

Lori turned to Julian. "You said you can get respirators. Can you really do that?"

"I know I can," he said dryly. "One of my buddies is a prepper. He's got a basement full of stuff for his family, just in case the world blows up."

"So we're doing this?" Amy asked, then held her breath.

Julian rubbed his chin, forehead wrinkling. "I don't know. Shouldn't we tell the police? It doesn't feel right to hold back information like that."

Amy snorted. "Kyle already went to the police, told them everything. He might as well have been talking to a wall."

Lori grabbed Julian's shoulders and spun him around until their noses were inches apart. "And what have they done to find Maria, except make excuses? You heard Amy. They're too busy trying to hide the fact they haven't even done a thorough search."

Julian sighed. "Maybe. All right. Yeah."

Amy's eyes flicked upward in relief. She watched him cross to the sink and pour a glass of water. He'd just finished gulping it down when he leaned forward and yanked down the blinds.

"There's a man on the other side of the garden wall."

Amy's pulse quickened.

"Maybe he was walking by," Lori said, voice low. "The trail goes right by there."

Julian shook his head. "No. He was just standing there. Watching."

Amy paced across the kitchen. How long had the guy been following her? Probably since she visited Gabriele Bruno, who must have been connected to Maria and whatever was going on.

Julian marched toward the back door, determined footsteps echoing through the room.

Amy raced after him, grabbing his arm when his hand reached the doorknob. "Wait, Julian! This is a bad idea."

But Julian didn't listen. He flung open the door, hinges creaking in protest, and charged toward the man lurking in the distance. Amy ran after him, breathless, and saw the man freeze before turning and scurrying away. Julian catapulted himself over the wall and followed.

Muttering under her breath, Amy ran out of the gate, stepping onto the headland for the first time. No trees. No places to hide. Just a network of dirt paths, a few figures in the distance, some dogs, and a breathtaking view of the Pacific Ocean. No sign of the two men. Amy wondered what Julian would do if he caught the man. Lori ran up, her chest heaving.

"Where do you think they went?" Amy asked.

Lori scanned the area, hands jammed under her armpits. "Probably into the neighborhood."

They didn't have to wait long to find out. Moments later, Julian appeared, face flushed, panting.

"He got away. There was a car waiting."

"Was it a silver four-door?"

"No. It was a small black car."

Amy's mouth went dry. Not one, but two people had been assigned to watch them. Probably to figure out what she knew. Maybe to keep her quiet. They must have been following her all day.

"Is there a way we can get to the kilns without parking in one of the lots?" Suddenly, staying under the radar seemed a top priority.

Julian shot Lori a quick glance. They both nodded.

"Yeah," Julian said. "The way we used to go. It's a longer drive, but it cuts down the hike time."

Amy had never hiked in her life, but she wasn't about to let them know that. "We need to get going before they come back."

Julian hurried off to fetch the respirators and his daypack, leaving Amy to help Lori search the storage room off the garage for the camping gear they'd need.

"The tent's got to be here somewhere," Lori muttered, shoving aside a stack of clear bins.

Amy froze. "We have to stay overnight?" Hiking might be okay, but camping was an experience she'd so far managed to avoid.

With a triumphant cry, Lori snatched a green bundle from the back of a shelf and straightened. She clutched it to her chest and gave Amy a worried look. "I don't think you really understand just how long it takes to get to the kilns."

Chapter 28

David relished the solitude of his house. It was just as he preferred it. No pesky manager popping in to offer unsolicited advice, no caretakers invading his private space. He'd even given Anita a month off with pay to buy himself some time.

And he'd ignored yet another call from his doctor, asking him to come in for more tests.

At his last visit to the neurologist, David had held his head high and moved without a walker. The doctor was astounded. He performed a thorough examination and asked dozens of questions before stepping back, shaking his head.

"A spontaneous remission is completely unprecedented."

David had merely shrugged. "Well, maybe it was a misdiagnosis, then. You wouldn't be the first doctor to get things wrong."

A text message followed: We've scheduled a brain scan.

David had sighed and tapped a reply: No thank you. I'll be in contact if I change my mind.

The doctor couldn't compel him to take any more tests. In fact, there was no further need of the specialist's services.

But David did need something. A new company. One to carry out his new mission. He spent the rest of the morning on the phone with lawyers.

It would be an entirely new venture. An international enterprise. It would require serious funding, but that wasn't a problem. He had money, and suddenly, miraculously, he had the health and energy to make it all happen.

David would be the CEO, of course. And he had a lot of work to do. Buildings to build, substrate to test, employees to hire and train. More human trials. And eventually, a public announcement, marketing, and distribution.

But for now, it was a startup, a situation David had been in many times, one he found exhilarating.

When the calls with his lawyers ended, David unpacked the boxes of outdoor gear he'd had delivered. There was no telling how long he'd be gone, but he wanted to be warm and comfortable. David might have recovered from crippling dementia, but he didn't have superpowers. He was still a fifty-nine-year-old man who'd spent more time behind a desk than wandering the forest.

David pulled on a new pair of wool socks, then tried on several hiking boots. He ran up and down the stairs a few times to test the fit. The stairwell smelled faintly of radishes, but he didn't mind. The purple and rosy mushrooms growing from the walls were quite pretty, and he liked their name too—Lilac Bonnet.

He knew the names of all the fungus in his house.

The Fringed Crumble Cap and Sulfur Tuft grew near the back door. The Yellow Stainer sprouted in the meadow and in a corner of his office. The pale violet Blewitt had taken over the pantry. But of all the varieties flourishing inside his house, the funnel-shaped Chanterelles, with their pale orange skin and faint scent of apricot, were his favorites. They surrounded his bed. Normally, they didn't appear until July, but growing seasons didn't seem to matter.

The mushrooms came because they had been sent, and that was good enough for David.

Chapter 29

They reached the top of yet another hill, and Lori wiped the sweat from her forehead. They hadn't gone that far, and the air was chilly, but the terrain was rugged.

Lori ran regularly but avoided the hills, and she was paying for it now. "I thought I was in pretty good shape, but wow. I guess I'm not as young as I used to be."

Julian shot her a sidelong smirk, eyebrows lifted. "You look in pretty good shape to me." Then glanced away, clearing his throat. "I'm feeling it too. Work on the ranch doesn't require this much cardio."

"Are you sure this is the right trail? It doesn't look familiar at all."

"I'm sure. It's been a long time, but it's the same trail we always took."

Lori couldn't help but wonder if trauma had altered her memory or if the windstorm which had felled so many trees had destroyed familiar landmarks.

She had plenty of time to think. And worry.

Just because she and Julian were desperate to find Maria didn't mean Maria wanted to be found. In fact, all evidence pointed to the contrary. Maria was an adult. Why would she listen to parents who were strangers? Especially Lori.

But they had to try to find out what was going on. They owed her that, at least.

Amy's enthusiasm had faded as soon as they started hiking. She'd already tripped a few times, and once she lagged so far behind, Julian had to backtrack and get her. Her hair seemed to act as a magnet for twigs and debris, and the knees of her jeans were caked in mud.

They made their way in silence through the woods until they reached a massive rock encircled by trees. The trio paused to rest and eat some of the sandwiches Lori had packed. Amy stretched out and fell asleep.

Lori and Julian exchanged uneasy glances. The young woman was exhausted. And the most difficult parts of the hike were still ahead. They had warned her about the rugged terrain, but she'd been determined, almost driven, to join them.

After twenty minutes, Julian tapped the bottom of Amy's boot.

"Cat nap is over, princess. Time to go."

Amy woke with a groan. "Jesus. I have to pee." She looked around as if expecting a bathroom to materialize.

Lori sighed, fished a roll of toilet paper from her backpack, and guided a grumbling Amy to a spot just out of view.

Amy lowered herself into position. "Please don't leave. I don't want to get attacked by a bear or something." She moaned. "Jesus. I hope I don't get poison oak on my vag."

Lori couldn't help but laugh. "That's all you need."

"That ever happen to you?" Amy peered up at her with wide, nervous eyes.

"No, because I know what it looks like and I wouldn't squat over it, and I wouldn't let you either."

While she waited for Amy to finish her business, which seemed to take forever, a thought struck Lori. After they'd made their way back to Julian, she said, "The search crews probably didn't make it much farther than this. In fact, they may not have made it *this* far. But they were sick enough to call off the search. So why are we okay?"

Julian stared into the woods and took a deep breath. "I have no idea. I figured we'd know when we needed to put on the respirators. Like, we'd start feeling sick or dizzy or something. But we're fine. And I really don't know why."

A few minutes farther down the trail, the trees thickened and blocked out the cloudy sky. The occasional drop of rain fell on Lori's face. In the fading light, they navigated a series of steep inclines. The leaves were slippery, even causing sure-footed Julian to slide while they climbed yet another hill.

Darkness fell rapidly in Nils Forest, and soon, they had to rely on their flashlights. They trudged on for a half hour until they reached another hill.

"Are you kidding me?" Amy cried.

Lori grabbed Amy's hand, intending to pull her along, but her foot came down on a rock, and Lori's ankle rolled. A jolt of pain shot up her leg, and she fell with a gasp. Julian knelt beside her, so close the hair on his head touched her chin. His cool, strong fingers explored her ankle. She winced and bit her lip. It hurt, but it wasn't broken.

"Can you stand?" His voice was filled with concern.

Lori nodded. "I think so."

Julian stood, grabbed both of her hands, and pulled her to her feet. She took a tentative step and winced again. Her ankle throbbed, but the stabbing pain was gone.

Amy stood to the side, biting her thumbnail and muttering, "Shit, shit, shit."

"Calm down," Lori said sternly. "It's just a mild sprain."

Julian studied her in the gloom. "Are you sure?"

Lori shrugged. "We'll find out soon enough." She took a few hobbling steps and found it wasn't nearly as bad as she had feared. Julian took her arm, and she didn't protest. Amy followed close on their heels.

They pulled up the hoods on their jackets when it began to drizzle again. Rain wasn't something she and Julian had contended with all those years ago. Their time at the kilns had been during the summer, an unusually warm and dry one for Mendocino.

"Just a little farther," Julian said.

Lori turned to look at him. *What* was a little farther? There was no destination, no snug, warm hut waiting ahead. There was nothing but an obstacle course of trees, ravines, and creeks between them and the kilns.

"Are we even going in the right direction?" Amy finally asked after a long silence.

Even if it were daylight, Lori couldn't be sure, so she said nothing. The rain only added to her mounting sense of disorientation.

"We are," Julian replied after a moment.

Lori hoped he was right. Getting lost in Nils Forest was something they hadn't considered.

She'd lost track of time. It was probably six o'clock, but it felt like midnight. Lori could dig out her phone to check the time, but what difference would it make? They were soaked and miserable, and she needed to rest her foot. Lori'd kill for a glass of wine and a hot bath. She was about to suggest they stop for the night when Julian came to an abrupt halt.

"Do you hear that?"

They froze.

At first, all Lori could hear was soft rain falling on leaves. But then, the sound of voices in the distance, like several people, and it was hard to tell where it was coming from.

Amy grabbed her arm. "We need to hide."

Lori turned to the woman in surprise. Amy's voice quivered. Her bravado was gone.

Julian put his finger to his lips. "Quiet. Turn off your flashlights. I think they're on the other side of the hill. You two stay here. I'm going up to have a look around."

Amy was shaking her head. "We need to stick together."

"Not with Lori's ankle. I can move faster on my own."

Lori swallowed. As much as she hated the idea of being left in the woods, at night, alone with Amy, Julian was right. And he wasn't going far.

"We'll be fine," Lori said, with more certainty than she felt.

Julian disappeared into the darkness. Lori and Amy crawled under a rocky outcropping. At least it was dry there.

After just a few minutes, Lori heard Amy's soft breathing as the girl nodded off, leaning against her.

Lori put an arm around the young woman's thin shoulders, a moment of intimacy she had never had a chance to share with her own daughter. She fought back the sudden flood of tears and swallowed through the knot in her throat. Her ankle continued to throb, and her body tensed. She strained to listen for the sound of Julian's return.

Then a thought hit her. They were close to a camp of some sort, and they still weren't sick. Except for her ankle, which was no mystery, they all felt just fine.

What was that about?

Finally, Julian appeared in the clearing, breathless. From the shadows, Lori threw a rock to get his attention. He jogged over to them and squatted next to her.

"There's a camp just over the hill," he said in a low voice. "A dozen tents, maybe."

"Did you see Maria?" Next to her, Amy stirred.

"No. There are a lot of people, though. And there's a big tent, like a dining hall or something. They have lanterns, so I could see outlines of people, but that's all."

It was too dark to make out Julian's face, but Lori could hear the tension in his voice.

"What did you see?" she whispered. "Tell me."

"I did recognize one person. The guy back at the house, the one looking in the window. He's there. Just standing at the edge of the camp, like he's waiting for something." Julian paused. "It's almost like they're expecting us."

Beside her, Amy's body gave a little twitch.

Lori's thoughts jumped around until an epiphany struck, making her ribs tighten.

Amy knew more than she'd told them.

That explained Amy's change in demeanor after they had entered the forest. It wasn't just the difficulty of the hike. Amy was afraid. Afraid of the people in the trees.

But why?

They decided to make camp hidden under the rocky overhang. Julian set up the tent, and they crawled inside, bumping elbows in the tight quarters. Amy ate a granola bar, slipped into her sleeping bag, and immediately dozed off, snoring softly. The girl, it seemed, could sleep anywhere.

Lori crawled into her sleeping bag, and Julian gently zipped it up, pressing a soft kiss on her forehead. In that moment, she longed to confide in him about Amy, to speculate on her motives and her secrets. But Lori was too exhausted. She closed her eyes and drifted off, her thoughts turning to Maria.

Chapter 30

Julian was still asleep, his head poking out from the top of his sleeping bag. Amy was turned toward Lori, face pale in the morning light.

Lori gazed at her, willing her to wake. A few moments later, the young woman's eyes fluttered open.

Lori had spent the last hour thinking. And the more she contemplated, the more convinced she became Amy had lied to them.

"What didn't you tell us?" she whispered.

The rain had finally stopped, but water droplets continued to slide off the trees above and pelt the tent in a steady drip.

Amy gave a little groan. "Good morning to you too."

"I'm serious, Amy," she hissed. "If there's something you're holding back, you need to tell me."

Lori glanced over at Julian. He hadn't even stirred. Apparently, he was a heavy sleeper. It was amazing how much she didn't know about him.

Amy struggled to sit. "Oh God. I feel like crap."

The young woman's complexion appeared waxy, and her buggy eyes were dull. Maybe she was coming down with something. If so, the timing couldn't be worse. Lori rummaged through a compartment in her daypack and pulled out a bottle of ibuprofen. Amy shook out two tablets and swallowed them dry.

"Well?"

Amy's eyes darted around the tent as if searching for an escape.

Finally, she spoke, her voice barely above a whisper. "So yeah. There's stuff I didn't tell you because I was afraid you wouldn't come."

Lori pressed a palm against her forehead. What had Amy left out? Whatever it was, Julian had to hear it too. She nudged him until he stirred, then tapped him on the shoulder a few times until he sat up in his sleeping bag with a yawn.

"What is it?"

"Amy has something to tell us."

That got Julian's attention. He grimaced. "All right. Let's hear it."

Amy propped herself up on an elbow. "Well, it's actually a lot." She paused, sighing heavily. "Those people out there? They're not just some hippy-dippy mushroom group. It's a cult. And their leader is someone they call the Spore Queen. You heard what Maria said on the recording about the sky opening up and revealing a new god? I think we can safely assume these mushroom people worship that new god."

Amy broke eye contact.

Lori's mind reeled, struggling to make sense of Amy's words. A slow, icy tingle moved up her spine. "The Spore Queen. Who is she?"

Julian's head swiveled toward her. "It can't be."

When Amy shrugged, Lori wanted to scream. Instead, through gritted teeth, she forced out the words, "You said you thought Maria was dead, and now you're saying you think it's possible she's this Spore Queen?"

"I don't know. Maybe. It could be anyone, honestly." Amy grimaced. "But that's the least of our worries. The guy I talked to, the one who escaped, he was scared shitless. He saw a lot of stuff go down. Bad stuff. A new recruit refused to take a ceremonial mushroom, and he disappeared, and then there was some sort of ritual, and the man leading it was wearing an animal skin."

Julian scrambled out of his sleeping bag and crouched, glaring at Amy and rolling it up. "That's what he said? Are you sure that's what he said? A ceremonial mushroom?"

Amy plucked at a loose thread on the sleeve of her sweatshirt. "Yeah. That's not a detail I'd get wrong." Her voice was faint.

Julian sank back onto his heels, shaking his head, a far off look in eyes. "Just like Maria said."

A cold iron band squeezed Lori's chest, making it hard to breathe. "What makes you think Maria might be this Spore Queen? Do you have any evidence?"

Amy bit her lip. "No, but you heard her. She was talking about her people and how she needed to make a plan. If I'm being totally honest, I wouldn't be all that surprised."

Lori heard it then. The tone—the disdain shot through with resentment. She leaned forward and grabbed Amy's hand. "You don't like my daughter, do you?"

Amy gave a little shrug. "She was good to me. Generous. But she wasn't always easy to like. She was…" Her voice drifted off.

Whatever it was, however hard it was to hear, Lori had to know.

"She was what?" Lori pressed, voice rising.

Amy's buggy eyes regarded Lori with a mixture of sadness and regret. "Smart. Beautiful. Entitled. Spoiled. And often very clueless."

Every word was like a dagger to Lori's heart. "You're not here to help us find her, are you? You're not here because you're worried about your friend?"

Amy was silent for a long time, frowning as if considering whether to answer or if another lie was in order.

"No," she finally said. "I'm a reporter. You knew that. I'm sorry. I'm here for a story."

She paused to clear her throat.

"And there's something else you don't know. Maria was diagnosed with Hodgkin's lymphoma last year, but they caught it early. She had to do some treatments, and she ended up fine, but for a while there, she was freaking out, trying to decide whether she wanted to be cremated or buried under a tree. The next thing I knew, she'd made a will and told me she left her apartment to me."

Lori recoiled, waves of confusion washing over her. The revelation felt like a betrayal. "How could you not have told us that?" Her voice quivered.

Her daughter had been through a scary, traumatic experience, and Lori had never known a thing. And with sudden clarity, Lori realized something else.

"You can't inherit the place unless you can prove Maria's dead. Otherwise, you'd have to wait years! *That's* why you're here."

Amy tipped her head back and gave a little moan. "You don't know what it's like to be poor, like me, working in a job that pays in prestige but not enough money to live. Besides, Maria wanted me to have it." Amy fell back onto her sleeping bag and stared up at the tent. Her body began to shake, like she was starting to cry. She clasped her stomach.

"Are you okay?" Julian asked, voice tinged with alarm.

Amy didn't respond. Instead, she leaned over and vomited into a corner of the tent.

Chapter 31

"Oh, man. Let's get some air in here." Julian moved toward the flap, glancing at Amy's crumpled form. He slid the zipper up and over the flap, then pulled the nylon fabric through the opening.

"Whoa!"

Lori looked out over his shoulder. "Oh, wow."

Mushrooms surrounded their tent. A startling variety of shapes, colors, and sizes formed a neat half-moon around the opening. The only ones Lori could name were the morels, with their strange, pitted caps, but there were dozens of others.

Julian silently gestured toward a line of pale threads emerging from behind a group of saplings and leading to the tent. They disappeared beneath the section of nylon closest to Amy.

Lori spun around and crawled over to the helpless girl, who was now bent over and retching in the corner again. She grabbed Amy's arm and dragged her to the other side of the tent, putting some distance between her and the threads. Amy was too sick to resist.

With a flick of her wrist, Lori tossed Amy's sleeping bag aside. Hairy white filaments had wound themselves around the underside.

In a sudden moment of clarity, Lori realized their mistake. No one had fallen ill on their hike, and they'd become complacent. But it was just a matter of time before they got sick too.

"Get the respirators," she said to Julian.

His eyes widened in understanding, and he quickly retrieved them from his day pack.

Lori put her respirator on, then watched Julian strap his over his head and crawl toward Amy. She patted his arm and gestured for him to wait. Lori grabbed a cloth from her backpack, poured some water from her canteen, and wiped Amy's face and mouth.

Amy resisted when Julian tried to help her with the respirator, but she quickly gave up, seeming to understand its necessity. Lori hoped Amy wouldn't throw up in the mask.

They'd thought their makeshift camping spot had been ideal, but they needed to find somewhere else for Amy to recover. Somewhere free of the mushrooms Lori was sure were making Amy sick. Julian led them down an embankment toward a small creek, Amy supported between them, away from the people camped on the other side of the hill.

While Julian left to search for another site, Lori did her best to clean the vomit from Amy's hair and neck with fresh water from the creek. After that, she helped Amy change into a clean sweatshirt. With the rain and mud, they were churning through clothes at an alarming rate. At least the rain had stopped. She could see the gray sky through the trees.

After a short time, Julian returned and guided them down a gentle slope until they reached a cluster of massive boulders. Two colossal trees had fallen across the rocks, forming a covered space below big enough for their tent. An ideal hiding spot.

Amy sat, shoulders hunched, expression hidden, while Lori and Julian set up the tent.

Through the respirator, Amy said she wanted to go back into the tent, but Julian insisted they let it air out to give whatever had made Amy sick a chance to disperse. Amy groaned and stretched out on top of her sleeping bag, staring up at the trees listlessly.

It was too difficult to talk with the respirators over their faces, so Lori and Julian sat holding hands. A hundred thoughts rattled around in Lori's head. Learning Maria had had cancer was a shock, but it also helped explain why Maria had suddenly seemed to pull back from their relationship. She'd been too busy dealing with all of that. If only Maria had trusted Lori enough to confide in her. But why should she? What had Lori ever done to earn her daughter's trust?

Her thoughts drifted back to the mushrooms. She didn't know much about fungus, but there was nothing normal about the way the mushrooms had sprouted outside their tent. And Lori didn't think it was a coincidence Amy had gotten sick right after they sprouted. Either the mushrooms or the white fibers must have caused the nausea and disorientation, the same symptoms that had forced the search teams to turn back.

It seemed impossible, but had the mushroom cult people figured out how to use the fungus or its tendrils to make people sick? If so, it was selective. She and Julian were fine. What was different about Amy?

With a start, Amy sat up and looked around, rubbing the side of her face and blinking. Before they could stop her, she began frantically clawing at the respirator over her mouth. She ripped it off and threw it aside, gulping in fresh air.

"I can't stand it anymore!"

Eyebrows raised in concern, Lori watched Amy closely, expecting her to collapse again, but the young woman seemed fine. Her eyes were brighter, the pallor in her skin gone. After a few minutes, Lori glanced over at Julian and nodded. He hesitated for a moment, and together, they removed their respirators.

Lori took a few tentative, cautious breaths and waited. The air smelled of damp soil and pine. Clean. Fresh. Maybe whatever the mushrooms had released didn't have a scent.

"I think it's fine," Julian finally said, looking over at Amy.

Her hair was bunched up, giving her a startled appearance. "I'm better." She paused. "Thank you. For helping me."

A stiff nod was all Lori could manage.

Chapter 32

Lori was desperate for coffee. They'd left the propane behind, and starting a fire for the kettle was out of the question. The smoke would drift over the hill, giving away their location to those on the other side. For breakfast, they ate the bison jerky and biscuits Julian had packed. The biscuits were savory and delicious. Lori wasn't a big fan of jerky, but she was hungry and it was filling. Amy waved away the food.

After they finished, Julian began to pace. They hadn't talked about Amy's confession, not with her around, but it must have been troubling him too. He'd gone from discovering he had a daughter to fearing she was dead, to learning she might still be alive, to hearing she might be involved in a cult.

Lori hoped to God it wasn't true.

"I'm going to take a look around," Julian finally said. "Then we can decide what to do next." He shot a quick look at Amy, eyes narrowing. "I guess I should be on the lookout for violent nutjobs. You know, if you had bothered to tell us about all that sooner, we might have come better prepared. I've got a locker full of rifles I use for hunting. It would sure be nice to have one of those now, considering the circumstances."

Amy regarded him with dull eyes. "I know. I'm sorry."

Alarm twanged deep inside her chest. Things had changed dramatically since they entered the forest.

"Julian, we're in over our heads. We don't even know what we're dealing with or who these people are, or what they're capable of. Maybe we should go back. Get some help."

"Maybe," he replied, eyes fixed on the hill.

Lori tried again. "The police have got to believe us now. We'll tell them about the mushrooms, and they can send people out with respirators."

"Some photos would help," Amy said. "I've got a camera. It has a decent lens."

Julian swiveled around to face her, then held out his hand. "That's good. I'll take it with me. See what I can get."

"You're not going alone," Lori snapped. "I'm going too."

Julian frowned. "But your ankle."

"I'll wrap it."

The crease between Julian's eyes deepened. "It's a bad idea. What if we need to run?"

"Then I'll run."

Amy gave a weary laugh. "Would you two please go and let me take a nap?"

Julian pulled Lori toward him. "Don't you think you should stay here?" he asked in a low voice. His breath tickled her ear. "What if the mushrooms come back? What if she gets sick again?"

The question caught her by surprise. "That's not my problem. She brought this on herself."

Julian's eyebrows lifted. "Harsh."

"Maybe. But it's the truth. Besides, I want to take a look for myself. And I'm probably a better photographer."

After settling Amy in the tent, Lori wrapped a bandage around her swollen ankle, popped three ibuprofens, and joined Julian on the trail. The low-hanging gray fog had disappeared, but a layer of thin, wispy clouds still blocked the sun's rays.

Julian took her hand and pulled her up one hill, then another. They stopped when they reached a steep incline covered with brush and rocks. Just looking at it made her ankle throb.

Julian must have read her mind. "Are you up to this? You can stay here."

"I'm fine." The muscles in her legs tightened in readiness. "Let's go."

Scaling the hill was harder than it looked. The rain had turned the ground into a slippery slope of mud, but the rocks held, and she was able to use them to hoist herself up in the tricky areas. When they finally reached the ridge, Julian grabbed her arm, pulled her into a crouch, and guided her toward a thick tree.

Lori cautiously peered around it, making sure to stay hidden behind a row of ferns. She hadn't expected the camp to be so close, or for there to be so many people milling around.

There were men and women, from young adults to people older than herself. Some appeared to be in their mid-sixties. Lori wasn't sure how members of a cult dressed, but she'd imagined tie-dye and caftans. Instead, these people wore jeans, sweatshirts, and fleece jackets. It gave the impression of a clean, well-organized campsite, with people wearing lots of layers, prepared for the changeable weather.

"I don't think we can get a good picture without them seeing us," she whispered.

Wordlessly, he pointed at a deer trail across the top of the ridge. If they kept low, the ferns would provide cover. When they reached a safe distance from the camp, Julian stopped. Lori snapped a few photographs.

Julian pointed off to their left. "There's a path leading in this direction," he said in a low voice. "The kilns have got to be nearby. Are you still okay to walk?"

Lori nodded. The ibuprofen and the adrenaline had kicked in. "I'm fine." She was prepared to fake it, if necessary. "That camp. It's so well organized and seems to have plenty of provisions. How have all those people managed to avoid being found? It's…"

"Crazy." Julian finished her sentence with a scowl. "This isn't good, Lori. I know I don't need to tell you that. But it's seriously messed up. That whole thing about some guy wearing a deer skin and people tripping out on mushrooms? I don't like it."

Lori snorted. "I can't think of many people who would."

He was shaking his head before she finished. "Of course not. That's not what I mean. What I'm saying is, I've heard of it before. Stories from the days of the Spanish invading the Aztec empire, and even before that. I keep thinking about what Maria said, about learning stuff from my ancestors. Our ancestors. And now all these mushrooms. The Aztecs took psychedelic mushrooms too. I just don't like how this is starting to look, you know?"

Lori didn't. Not really. And now was not the time to talk about it. They needed to take more photos, the more incriminating the better, and get out of there.

After that, they needed to decide what to do next.

Julian's eyes were dark and pleading. He had always been good-looking, but with age, he'd grown into his features. Now he was rugged. Handsome. And loyal. She'd left him, given away the baby he didn't even know he had, and ignored him for more than two decades, and somehow, there he was, alongside her in the middle of the forest where they'd consummated their relationship all those years ago.

Lori touched his cheek. "Let's get our pictures and get out of here."

Julian pulled her to him, and for one heady moment, she was lost in his embrace, then they were on the move again. It took less than fifteen minutes to find the kilns, guided by loud voices and the distinct sound of nails being pounded into wood.

From atop a ridge, they spotted a clearing in front of the stone buildings. Tents ringed the open space. People were moving in and out of a cave. Men were constructing a triangular wooden structure, wider at the bottom, with narrow boards serving as steps.

Julian and Lori hid and watched the working men.

"What are they building?" she whispered.

Julian bit his lip. "I don't know."

A man emerged from the cave, middle-aged and dressed in a flannel shirt and baggy jeans. "Listen up, people," he shouted. "It's happening sooner than we thought. Tonight, not tomorrow, so let's get a move on."

With sudden clarity, Lori realized this was no small gathering of outcasts looking to get high in the forest. This group was organized, driven, and dangerous.

And Amy had known that all along.

Chapter 33

Amy had blown it. Again.

She was very good at weaponizing honesty.

Why? Why had she admitted her true feelings about Maria to Lori? Because Amy knew, at her core, she was a mean girl, full of envy and spite.

At least, that's what her mother had said, and her friends too. Well, her *ex*-friends. She seemed to fall out with people quickly, mostly because she pushed them away if they got too close. Especially if those people came from better circumstances. The fact was, Amy couldn't stand to be around women who had all the advantages she lacked: doting parents, a nice house, family money.

Maria had been the only one who hadn't cut her off, and yet Amy'd insulted her to her mother's face. Why couldn't she keep her mouth shut? She'd lost Lori's trust and earned her suspicion at the worst possible time—stuck out in the middle of the forest, surrounded by fucking mushroom lunatics.

Had those mushrooms really made her sick? And had they made her a little dizzy? Maybe a *lot* dizzy? Had she been hallucinating, or had she seen the mushrooms outside the tent swaying on their stems while Lori and Julian dragged her outside?

Amy anxiously scanned their small campsite for more fungus, but so far, none had appeared. She couldn't remember ever feeling so disoriented, so sick, not even when she'd had a bad case of the flu in college. But she felt better. At least, physically.

Her stomach rumbled. She hadn't eaten anything since that sandwich yesterday. The biscuits and bison jerky in Julian's day pack were an option, but it felt wrong to go through his stuff. Then again, she was starving, and who knew when they would come back?

She had to hand it to the guy. Julian had brought along enough food to last for several days. In fact, between him and Lori, they seemed to have thought of everything for their jaunt into the forest. Lori had even packed rags and wipes for cleaning.

Amy ate two biscuits. They were surprisingly good. Of course, anything loaded with butter and chives was bound to be delicious. She nibbled a piece of jerky but, halfway through, tossed it aside. It was too much work to chew the stuff. A hot mug of soup would have been amazing, but Julian had said starting a fire was out of the question.

There wasn't anything to do but sit and stare at the trees. Did Nils Forest have bears? Mountain lions? Lori might have been happy to leave her alone with wild animals prowling around, but Julian would certainly have warned her.

Then again, he had been busy and preoccupied so might have forgotten to mention it. Did you make yourself big and shout if you saw a bear, or avoid looking directly at them? Amy never could remember. It wasn't something she had to worry about in San Francisco, although she had once seen a coyote loping through Golden Gate Park at dusk.

The sound of approaching footsteps made her jump. Amy whirled around, half expecting to see the man who'd followed her in town, but it was only Julian and Lori.

"Did you find anything?"

Lori pursed her mouth as if determined not to say anything, but Julian nodded. "We found the kilns. These people are really organized, and it looks like they're building some sort of scaffolding. They're getting ready for an event tonight."

An icy finger ran down Amy's spine. "Like what?"

Lori shook her head. "We don't know. Something they'd had scheduled for tomorrow, but they moved it up. We didn't exactly feel like sticking around too much longer."

"Did you get any pictures?"

"A few. I wouldn't call them shocking, though."

"Give me the camera." Amy put her hand out. "I want to see what you got."

Lori handed her the camera, and Amy scrolled through the pictures, staring at the small screen.

"You're right. These are boring. It looks like a fucking scout camp," she scoffed. Amy took a moment to consider her options. If the photos had shown some creepy cult activities, Lori and Julian would have probably been in a hurry to show them to the police. These weren't good enough to get anybody's attention.

However, whatever was happening tonight sounded interesting. Pictures of some weird ritual would make for a big splashy exclusive. And hopefully, Maria would make an appearance.

"We need to be there tonight. For whatever it is they're doing," she said. "We need those pictures."

Julian and Lori exchanged uneasy glances. It hadn't escaped Amy's attention that, on the hike, they'd acted like a couple. Holding hands. Talking quietly, heads bent together. The way they sneaked looks at each other. Not for the first time, Amy wondered if the two were now an official couple or if they were just working together for the sake of their daughter, with the occasional screw to liven things up.

"Are you up to it?" Julian asked, frowning.

"I'm fine now," she said.

"Okay, then, that's our plan. Let's be ready to leave in about an hour."

Lori didn't reply but patted his arm.

Once again, Amy realized how fortunate Maria was. Amy couldn't imagine her own parents coming to her rescue. They hadn't even bothered to send her a hundred bucks during her four years at college. And they had never asked if her measly scholarships were enough to cover the bills.

Sometimes, just thinking about it drained all her energy. It seemed so unfair Maria had not one, but three parents who loved her and rich grandparents to foot her bills, while Amy had to make her way alone in the world.

Lori and Julian started packing, when Amy noticed a patch of white near a fallen log. It hadn't been there before. She went over for a closer look—a ring of mushrooms surrounding a pile of loose dirt. Something was pushing its way up from the ground.

Pulse racing, Amy watched the dirt fall away, revealing a perfectly round mushroom with a bright red cap and white dots. It looked like something out of a fairy tale. It rose from the ground, its white stalk bending toward her.

A startled squawk escaped her throat. She jumped back, stumbled, and landed hard. White hairy fibers emerged from the mushroom ring and began slithering toward her. Her legs turned to stone, and she was powerless to move, the threads closing the gap between them.

A heavy boot landed in front of her, followed by another, crushing the threads beneath thick soles before shoving them out of the way. Strong hands hauled her to her feet.

It was Julian.

"We need to move. C'mon, let's go."

Lori handed over Amy's backpack, eyebrows knitting. "I don't know what's going on with that stuff, but you need to be extra careful. Those things don't seem to like you."

Chapter 34

Hills. So many hills. They just kept coming, and Amy wanted to cry.

Julian had to haul her up the steep incline to the ridge above the kilns. It was dark and hard to see. Going through a caffeine withdrawal wasn't helping matters. Plus, she was bloated from the peanut butter in the granola bar she'd eaten before they set off.

"I think I'm gonna die," Amy repeated over and over.

Lori paused long enough to pat her arm, her expression softening for the first time since Amy's big confession. "No, you're not. You're going to be fine. We're almost there."

The camera hanging from its strap bumped against Amy's chest, a reminder of her job ahead. She had to focus. *Get the incriminating photos and get the hell out of there, back to civilization, coffee, and hot food.*

When they were in position behind a row of boulders and brush, Amy could see about a dozen figures scurrying below in a clearing lit by torches on all sides. At the center of all the activity was an enormous pyramid made of wood, covered in earth.

"They've finished it," Julian whispered. He sounded worried.

Then, one by one, people began to walk out of the cave and surround the tall structure. With trembling fingers, Amy popped the cap off the lens and readied the camera. She turned off the flash and looked through the viewfinder. The light wasn't optimal, but it should work, and a photo expert could fix it later.

The people forming a circle around the pyramid talked excitedly amongst themselves, but Amy was too far away to hear them. From somewhere, a drum began to beat, slowly and steadily.

Amy rolled her eyes. These people liked their ceremonies with a little drama. She could feel the tension in the air while Lori and Julian watched, necks craned, bodies rigid with anticipation. Amy forced her attention back to the clearing and began counting the number of attendees, which was difficult because they were constantly moving.

Some of them seemed to be avoiding the structure and kept to the shadows of the trees, glancing around nervously. Apparently, not everyone was down with whatever was about to happen.

The drum beat quickened.

"She's here," a man shouted from below.

Amy's heart started up like a jackhammer. Was "she" Maria?

Julian clutched Lori's arm as if he expected her to dash down the hill.

The chatter stopped. Three figures emerged from the cave. Two women wearing long dark dresses. Their heads were bare, hair tied back in long single braids hanging down their backs.

The third woman was Maria. Even if Amy hadn't recognized her, Lori's sudden intake of breath announced her arrival as if Lori'd shouted Maria's name.

Her dress was simple, deep red without trim or adornment. It flowed to her ankles, just above her bare feet. Amy was so mesmerized by the unfolding spectacle, she only remembered the camera in her hands when Julian poked her in the side. She gazed through the viewfinder and adjusted the zoom lens.

Definitely Maria. But Maria had changed. Her honey blonde hair was longer, wilder. Her brown skin had paled, and her features had somehow become more pronounced. The bridge above her nose was more prominent, almost regal. The resemblance between Maria and her father was striking, and yet there was something about the wideness of her mouth and set of her chin that was all Lori.

Maria had become an ethereal beauty who commanded attention.

To the low beat of drums, the women walked toward the structure. Maria raised her head to the sky while her companions stared fixedly at the ground.

A murmur rippled through the crowd. Finally, the words loud and distinct enough for Amy to hear: *"The Spore Queen. The Spore Queen. Our Spore Queen."*

A figure darted out of the cave and hurried toward Maria. Amy immediately recognized the dark curly hair and handsome face—Gabriele Bruno, clutching a paper bag. He ran toward Maria until they were facing each other. Maria held out a hand, palm facing upward. Gabriele placed something on it too small for Amy to see, even with the magnification of the lens.

"Take it. Take it. Take it," the crowd chanted.

And Maria did. Without hesitation. From her vantage point, Amy couldn't see Maria's expression, but could imagine it. Smug. Victorious. The center of attention. A queen with her own cult.

Gabriele gave an awkward little bow, then jogged back toward the cave.

A loud metallic sound overhead made Amy jump. Something between a thunder clap and a giant zipper opening.

It repeated, becoming louder, more intense, and then there was a deafening clanging. A flash of lightning followed and a sudden torrent of rain. It fell directly on the clearing below but stopped at the edges of the trees.

Maria raised her hands above her head, face tilted to the sky.

Amy's hands were shaking now. She pressed her eye against the viewfinder, her finger automatically hitting the button. The people below were staring up at the sky, mouths open to the rain, hands held up as if in supplication. What were they looking at?

From their position on the ridge, Amy couldn't see.

Everyone in the crowd wore a dazed expression. Like they were in a trance. They must have been high.

Her attention shifted to Maria. She was swaying, hair lifting from her shoulders, feet coming off the ground. Jesus. Was she actually levitating? Amy looked through the viewfinder again, focusing on the area above Maria's shoulders, frantically searching for wires. If they existed, they were too thin to see.

Fuck.

The isolated storm on top of the crowd intensified. Hail fell from the sky. People threw their hands over their heads but made no move to run for cover. The hail dropped in a circle around Maria, but the chunks of ice didn't touch her, and she didn't flinch.

Another clang, louder than the others, sounded above them.

And then, Amy realized the pyramid had been made from more than wood and dirt.

"Mushrooms," Julian said in a hushed voice beside her.

Mushrooms covered nearly the entire structure. Brown, gray, red, green, purple, yellow, orange. They reminded Amy of a float covered in flowers. Strange. Beautiful. Disturbing.

The hail stopped as abruptly as it had started. The clanging noise ceased, replaced by an ominous low rumble in the sky, the vibration penetrating deep into Amy's bones.

Two men rushed forward with a wooden ladder and leaned it against the pyramid. Maria climbed until she reached a platform at the top, stopping next to a wooden table.

The rain continued to fall. Maria seemed oblivious to the elements and the noise.

A chill rippled down Amy's spine. The rain, falling in a tight circle, added to her unease.

Maria turned toward the group below. She threw her head back, her face illuminated by flashes of lightning. In a guttural voice that sent a shudder through Amy, Maria cried out into the darkness above.

Her wail was answered by a bone-chilling howl echoing through the night sky.

Chapter 35

Amy had nearly forgotten about Julian and Lori crouched beside her. It was so dark she couldn't see their faces, but she could sense their shock. Julian was rocking back and forth, Lori clinging to him, pressed into his side.

Fear gave off a musky smell, and the wet air was thick with it.

The horrible howls from the night sky ceased. The people in the clearing below slowly removed their hands from their ears. A few had dropped to their knees, while others lay face down in the mud.

Maria bent and picked several enormous mushrooms growing on a thick stalk, then threw them to a tall man holding a large basket below. He wore an elaborate deer mask and jacket with an upturned collar.

The group assembled around him, forming a line with their heads down and hands clasped together. With great solemnity, the man broke the mushrooms into smaller pieces and distributed them to the eager recipients. Not everyone joined the line. The two guys with shaggy hair, who appeared to be in their twenties, were doing their best to slink away unnoticed.

Two guards rushed over and forcefully pulled them to the back of the line. The men struggled against their grasps, shaking their heads in protest. For their efforts, they received rough shoves toward the man in the deer mask. Clearly panicked, the young men looked around before their gazes settled on the platform above. Maria stood at the edge, looking down at them, and pointed a finger in their direction.

Then, she raised her hand toward the sky in a simple yet threatening gesture.

The young men cowered but quickly recovered and snatched the offered mushroom pieces. They slunk away, shoulders slumped, to join the others. Some people sat cross-legged on the ground. Others held hands. A few formed small groups, standing in circles. On the platform, Maria sat too.

"What are they doing?" Amy whispered.

"Waiting for the psilocybin to take effect," Julian said in a low voice. "The magic mushrooms."

The evening had taken on a nightmarish quality. A steady, miserable, bone-chilling drizzle had begun to fall.

"How long will *that* take?"

"A while," Julian said with a certainty spoken from experience. "An hour, maybe."

Amy bit her bottom lip so hard she tasted blood. "Are you fucking kidding me? What are they going to do? Just sit there?"

"Looks like it."

Amy wanted to kick something. Her legs ached from crouching. She couldn't stay in that position another five minutes, let alone an hour. At least her rain jacket was long enough to cover her butt. She yanked it down, then sat on the ground and buried her head in her hands, muttering.

The time passed with agonizing slowness.

Amy had nearly drifted off when Julian nudged her. "They're starting."

She looked at the pyramid. Maria was no longer alone. Amy took in the lanky silhouette in the deer mask—a strange contrast with his outfit of jeans and bulky jacket—and an electric tingle shot down her spine.

Maria lifted her hands in the air, and the howls in the sky resumed. Below, people tipped their heads back, mouths falling open.

Maria began to speak. She had to shout to be heard over the ruckus. "Tonight, we're here to honor the arrival of an old god who I've reawakened with the help of a mushroom that is unlike any other. Those of you who've taken it, and are committed, will pass the test as you've done before, each time ascending to the next level of awareness. But those who are not committed, who do *not* believe, will fail and will serve as a sacrifice to the old god, reawakened and made new."

In response, people—now obviously high—stomped their feet and cheered. Some began to dance despite the lack of music, legs kicking, arms flailing. When Amy glanced over at Julian and Lori, they were both fully engrossed in the spectacle below, eyes wide, frightened.

The sight of the crowd's fervent response disgusted Amy. "For fuck's sake," she muttered.

Maria's words had an entirely different effect on the two young men who'd grudgingly eaten the psilocybin. They looked up at the sky, flung their arms over their heads, and began to convulse and contort. Their eyes rolled back in their heads, and they lurched toward the tents.

From the platform, Maria gazed down at them and pointed. "Disbelievers are among us," she thundered. "And they must go."

The effect was almost immediate.

Both men twitched and spasmed like they were performing a brutal dance. Their mouths twisted, trying to scream, and their hands flailed, reaching for someone to help them. They fell to the ground but continued to writhe and thrash. After a few moments, their bodies went rigid, frozen in a tangle of limbs. They stayed still like that for a few seconds, backs arched, arms and legs splayed in unnatural poses. Then their bodies went limp and collapsed to the ground.

The earth rumbled ominously. People scattered, some running toward the kilns, others for the trees.

A gust of wind swept through the clearing. Amy looked to the platform in time to watch mushrooms bursting from the edges. In seconds, they grew to an enormous size. Their pale flesh transformed into a vibrant red, glistening like strange hearts. Maria plucked them and arranged them on the table. With her hair swirling around her face, she waved her hands over the mushrooms as if casting a spell. The atmosphere around her seemed to ripple and shimmer. One by one, she tossed the mushrooms into the air.

Instead of dropping back down, they defied gravity and soared upward, like crimson butterflies.

A bolt of lightning illuminated the sky, followed by a deafening peal of thunder. The unearthly howl echoed through the night once more, filled with anguish and fury.

Then all was silent again.

Chapter 36

Lori jolted awake. Head pounding, sore all over, she sat up and looked around, confused. She was still on the ridge, wedged between a rock and some brush, Julian next to her, one arm flung over her waist. Amy was curled up in a ball, turned away from them. It was morning. The rain had stopped, droplets falling from the trees.

And then Lori remembered what had happened, and she wondered if she had dreamed it. She crawled through the brush and peered down into the clearing.

There was no sign of Maria.

Someone had taken away the two young men her daughter appeared to have condemned to death. Death by mushroom. But there were people down there, some lying on the ground, some stirring. A woman lurched to her feet and staggered to the bushes at the base of the hill where Lori hid. The sound of violent retching followed.

When Lori returned, Amy was propped up on one elbow, blinking, one side of her pale face blotchy with mud. Lori ignored her and crawled over to Julian, who was still fast asleep. It took several attempts to wake him, and when his eyes finally opened, they returned her gaze, dull and uncomprehending.

"I feel drugged."

Lori brushed a hand across his forehead. "Me too. I think we were. I think there was something in the air."

Amy staggered to her feet and looked around, inspecting the ground strewn with pine needles and twigs, peering behind rocks. After a few moments, she exhaled loudly and shook her head. "I don't see anything."

Lori pointed in the direction of the clearing. "There are still people down there."

Amy met her gaze, breathing raggedly. "We need to get out of here."

Lori returned her attention to Julian and crouched beside him, one hand resting on his shoulder. She pressed her mouth against his ear and said, "I don't remember falling asleep. Do you?"

His hand, the one resting on her knee, jerked. "No. But I remember everything else."

"Let's not talk about it here." Lori touched his cheek, then stood with some difficulty. Her legs were stiff from a night of sleeping on the wet, hard ground. Her pants were covered in mud.

Slowly, as quietly as they could manage, they picked their way down the steep slope toward their tent. Lori's ankle began to twinge halfway down.

The descent for Amy was more difficult than the climb up had been. She was grabbing at rocks and jutting branches to slow her progress. Just as she seemed to find some stability, Amy suddenly stumbled and fell to the side, one of her feet sunk into a muddy hole up to her knee. Julian spun around. Amy yanked her leg free with such force she was thrown off balance. Lori could only watch helplessly as Amy tumbled down the hill.

Julian hurried after her, but Lori remained perched on the slope, one hand over her mouth, following his progress. Only until he was safely at the bottom, leaning over Amy, did she continue to make her way down.

When Lori arrived at the bottom, heart racing, she took a closer look at the thin young woman. Somehow, Amy had managed to avoid slamming into any rocks or gashing herself on tree branches during her dramatic fall. She'd come through with scraped knees, elbows, and hands and several cuts on her face, including a bleeder on her forehead.

Lori plucked a twig from Amy's hair. "That was a bad one. You okay?" She found she couldn't stay mad at the young woman. Despite her deceit, hard edges, and bravado, there was something sad and vulnerable about Amy.

"Not really, but I'll survive." She stared up at Lori with remorseful eyes.

Julian pulled Amy to her feet, and they continued their journey back to their camp.

Once they reached their day packs, Lori attended to Amy's wounds in distracted silence, her thoughts drifting back to Maria on that platform. The way her feet had left the ground. The way Maria had pointed at those terrified young men. The mushrooms rising like birds into the air. And that screaming in the sky.

Had she dreamed it all? Or had it all been a hallucination caused by whatever drug had knocked them out?

Julian acted as sentry, pacing around, staring off into the trees. By the grim look on his face, Lori knew he, too, was haunted by what he'd seen.

Lori finished dressing the last of Amy's wounds and addressed Julian. "What do we do now?"

Amy's body gave an involuntary jerk, and she winced at the sudden movement. "What do you mean, what do we do? We get the hell out of here and go to the police."

Lori stared. "What about your story?"

Amy tentatively touched the bandage on her forehead and sucked in her breath. "I have the pictures, so I can start writing it when I get back to the house."

Lori wondered how much of that terrible ceremony Amy had managed to capture.

And did Lori even want to see the pictures? To see the evidence? Then she'd have to deal with it, with the knowledge her daughter was the leader of a cult, and she wasn't ready to accept that.

Denial was a cold comfort, but she'd take it until she no longer could.

Her chest hurt where it had pressed against the unforgiving ground. Or maybe she was having a heart attack. If she died, at least she wouldn't have to think about what her daughter had become.

Lori's thoughts spiraled into darkness, and the shock of last night's horrific events began to fade. She was vaguely aware of Julian and Amy arguing about what to do next.

And then Julian was standing next to her. "Why don't you go with Amy? Walk her back to the truck. I'll follow you in a while, but I want to see Maria first."

Lori leaned forward, folding her arms across her middle and forcing herself to breathe. She wanted to see Maria too. No matter what. "I'm coming with you. Amy can wait here until we get back."

Julian dug around in his daypack until he found what he was looking for. "These are to the truck. Just in case."

He tossed a set of keys to Amy, who made no attempt to catch them. They fell to the ground, just in front of her muddy boots. She stared down at them, mouth opening and closing.

"Are you fucking kidding me?" she finally asked.

Julian adjusted the straps on his backpack and didn't answer.

"Lori!" Amy's large eyes bulged. "Seriously?"

Lori went to her daypack and began pulling things out of it, adding them to Julian's. She tossed what was left in hers at Amy's feet. "I'm sorry, but I have to go. Maria is alive. We can't turn back now. You can take my pack. There's some water in there. And some food."

"You can't leave me out here by myself!" Amy's eyes were wild with panic. "If you don't return, I don't even know how to get back to the truck."

Julian cleared his throat. "You should be fine." He pointed. "Just head that way and you'll eventually come to the trail."

"I can't believe you still want to find her after what you saw," Amy shouted. "Your daughter is a fucking maniac."

Julian tipped his head back and sighed. "Maybe. But that's not all she is."

The ground seemed to drop beneath Lori's feet. "What do you mean?"

"She's a bruja." Julian was breathing through gritted teeth.

Amy was close enough to hear. "Not that bullshit again! You don't really believe that, do you? She's not a witch. She's running a Jim Jones con with killer mushrooms!" Spittle formed at the sides of her mouth.

Lori said nothing, mind reeling. Around her, the trees seemed to fade, the ground beneath her rolling. She felt herself slump against Julian, whose arm shot out and encircled her waist.

The rumble of voices made them freeze. People were coming. With a start, Lori looked around for someplace to hide, but it was too late.

From above the camp came a deep voice.

"Hello, Amy."

Chapter 37

Three men emerged from the thicket. Lori recognized two of them—the guards from the ceremony. They were even larger and more intimidating up close.

Amy took a giant step back, holding out her hands in front of her, warding them off. Her gaze shifted to the third man—nondescript, slightly paunchy.

"You were the one following me," Amy said, voice sharp with indignation.

The man gave an amused smile. "Guilty."

Beside her, Julian tensed, fists clenched at his sides. Lori clutched his arm. Julian was strong, but the men dwarfed him. The last thing she needed was for him to try to take them on. She stepped on his foot. Hard. He relaxed but only slightly.

The smaller of the two men had a large knife in a sheath hanging from his belt. The other was bald and sported a goatee.

"You found us," Lori mumbled, not knowing what else to say in such dire circumstances.

The knife man shrugged. He had a long nose set in a fleshy face. "I wouldn't say we *found* you. We knew you were here all along."

Lori didn't doubt it. The group had taken the trouble to follow Amy to her house. They'd been tracking them all the time. Even if she'd known, Lori wasn't sure what they could have done differently. The odds had been stacked against them as soon as they entered Nils Forest.

Lori's breaths were coming too fast. She bent over, hands on her knees, and her eyes flicked over the man.

He met her gaze, lip curled, and continued. "The Spore Queen knows everything that happens in this forest."

Amy rolled her eyes. "The Spore Queen? Really, dude? More like the Manson Family on 'shrooms." She snorted.

"You saw her," he growled.

Amy's eyes bulged. "I saw her. Yeah. Lots of drama. Probably some murder. And she's not the *Spore Queen*. Her name is Maria Hart. But hey, I'll give her this: she really puts on a good show."

Lori stared. Either Amy was able to hide her fear, or she was so outraged she was insensible to the danger these men presented.

The men glanced at each other, nostrils flaring. "You think the being in the sky was a show?" one snarled.

"Fuck if I know," Amy replied. "I didn't see what was making all that noise." She turned to Lori. "Did you?"

Lori was still finding it hard to breathe. The tightness around her throat had traveled downward. "No," she managed to say.

Beside her, Julian muttered, "I didn't have to."

Knife Guy grinned. "See? He knows. Daddy knows best."

Lori rubbed the center of her chest where the pressure had settled. So they knew. They knew Julian was Maria's father, which meant Maria had told them.

Amy threw her hands in the air and glared at Julian, hands landing on her hips. "You know what it sounded like to me? A giant ass speaker playing some bullshit spooky sounds. Come on."

Julian bit his lip and looked away.

Knife Guy took a step forward. Amy held her ground and met his gaze.

"Am I wrong? Then be my guest. Tell us what you think it was because I'm *dying* to hear this."

"New god," he said, grinning. The man simulated holding a guitar and pretended to strum. "Meet the new god, same as the old god."

The other men laughed.

Amy's eyes widened, and then she burst out laughing. "Oh wow. You're even bigger idiots than I thought. You do realize that song is called '*Won't Get Fooled Again,*' right?"

The smiles on the men's faces vanished, and Lori's heart sank. Amy had pushed it too far, and the men were all business again.

"All right, everybody," Knife Guy said. "We've wasted enough time. Let's go."

"Go where?" Julian demanded.

"Time to go see your baby girl," the paunchy man replied, then grabbed Amy by the arm and began marching her away.

Chapter 38

At least their captors let them change into dry clothes before taking them to the kilns. They also went through their packs, looking for weapons, but didn't confiscate anything.

The terrain began to look familiar to Lori in the daylight. Trees had come and gone, but the rocks and hills on the main path to the old stone buildings were the same. The memories came flooding back: Julian setting up camp, building a fire, pouring wine from a bota bag. The two of them talking, laughing, getting a little drunk, and making love as the embers cooled and the forest went still.

Then the mornings: washing in the cold creek, thick, steaming coffee made with an old kettle, and the long walk home.

There had been easier places to be alone, like the back of Julian's old junker of a truck, but once they'd discovered the kilns and the room behind them, there had been no other place that could compete.

But new memories now marred the old ones.

The guards held Amy tightly. They marched the cursing and exhausted reporter toward the encampment.

Lori and Julian followed. Whenever her thoughts drifted to the horrible ceremony they'd witnessed the night before and Maria's part in it, the tightness in her chest would return. Lori still hadn't told Julian about the panic attacks that had plagued her since surrendering Maria. Maybe she was too afraid to reveal that vulnerable part of herself, worried about how he would react.

And she still hadn't told him how little had changed since she gave Maria up. How she was still dependent on her parents for her livelihood, how her controlling father had become even more cruel and abusive.

After a few strenuous minutes, they reached their destination.

The kilns loomed above her. Up close, they were taller and more impressive than Lori had remembered. The three stone structures were covered in a layer of green moss. In front of them was a bustling center of activity. Tents, plastic tables, chairs, and cooking stations had been set up around the kilns, occupied by some of the people she recognized from the ceremony. But Maria was nowhere to be seen.

"Where's our daughter?" Julian asked, looking around.

The paunchy man said, "We just got here. How am I supposed to know? She'll see you when she's good and ready."

"How very queenish of her," Amy snapped.

"It's her right," he barked, giving her a little push toward the kilns.

Amy stumbled but managed to stay upright. "This is such bullshit."

The reporter's ashen face had taken on a sickly sheen. Despite being out of breath and hobbling, the march had not dampened Amy's rage. In fact, it appeared to intensify with each step.

Julian's thoughts were a complete mystery. He kept quiet and seemed entirely absorbed in his own private musings. Lori didn't know what to think. The details of last night's ceremony were already slipping away, and she struggled to hold onto her memories as the day went on. But those haunting noises in the night sky? Those she could still vividly recall.

Amy was convinced it had all been a performance, the loud noises blasting from hidden speakers and "rain" pouring out of hoses in the trees. And maybe she was right. Lori hoped so. Maybe it was all just an act, a horrific spectacle put on for the cult members. Maybe the victims were in on it, serving as actors in a grand illusion, all to convince people a new deity had come and Maria was the chosen leader. But where exactly was she leading them? What was the end goal of this charade?

The men ignored Amy's taunts. They led them past a group of people who stopped to stare, heads leaning together, talking quietly amongst themselves. There was nothing unusual about their appearances or anything to suggest they belonged to a cult.

The trio was taken into the middle kiln. The temperature immediately dropped. Unlike the last time Lori had been there with Julian, all the cobwebs and debris had been swept away, and lanterns lit the room, casting shadows on the uneven walls. There were card tables and camp chairs scattered around the room.

Julian took her arm, pulling her to his side. "Look," he whispered into her ear, jerking his head toward one of the walls.

A mural had been painted on the surface, an otherworldly landscape of mushrooms in bright colors. In the middle was a strange, squat figure resembling a gargoyle wearing a mushroom hat.

Amy stared up at it, blinking rapidly. She gave a quick high-pitched laugh, then looked away.

"Recognize it, do you?" The man's eyes fell on Amy's backpack, which she was now clutching to her chest.

Amy shook her head and lifted her chin. "It's trippy. If that's supposed to be your new god, I'd ask for an upgrade."

The warble in her voice told Lori the woman was rattled but trying hard not to show it.

The guard with the goatee stared down his nose at Amy, face expressionless, then cuffed her head, sending her sprawling. Before either Lori or Julian could react, he was dragging Amy through a door at the back of the room.

Years ago, the entrance to the back room had been hidden behind decrepit sheets of wood and a tangle of vines coming in through a hole in the roof. But all that was gone now.

Lori walked into the room, and her breath hitched in her throat. She took in the furnished bedroom. Cots covered in sleeping bags had been pushed together in a corner. Several low camp chairs surrounded an overturned crate draped with a striped blanket. There was a folding table too, with pale mushrooms growing out of a block of soil in a glass container.

Lori's eyes were drawn to a red dress draped over a chair. The dress Maria had worn during the ceremony.

Amy's rough treatment seemed to have fueled her anger, and the rude remarks continued to stream out of her mouth. Was she intentionally trying to goad their captors? Julian reached out and squeezed Amy's arm with a meaningful shake of his head, but she shook him off with a roll of her eyes.

"Wait here," the man with the goatee said. "We'll be right outside. Don't touch anything."

And with that, he was gone.

Without a word, Amy slumped her shoulders, and she staggered toward the cots. After tugging off her hiking boots with a groan, she fell back, arms flung over her face.

Lori and Julian exchanged uneasy glances. There was nothing else to do but wait. They might as well be comfortable. They settled onto the camp chairs. There was no heat in the room, and it was chilly. Julian found a blanket in a plastic bin and draped it over Lori's lap. In an instant, she felt drained, numb, and tired.

Julian's head was tilted back, eyes staring upward. Lori followed his gaze. The ceiling was covered in crude drawings of the gargoyle with the mushroom hat. Maria had been conceived in the cavernous space twenty-seven years ago. The drawings hadn't been there back then.

"What the hell, Julian?" she whispered.

When he finally turned toward her, his face was grim. "This is bad, Lori. I wish to god you'd never told her about my family history."

"What's that got to do with this?"

He rubbed the side of his face. "Everything. I told you, Maria's smart. She obviously did her research. My grandfather always said we came from a long line of brujos, all the way back to the Aztecs. I thought they were just cool stories, something he liked to say because he was proud of our culture. And I got really into it too. But the more I learned, the more I began to wonder if he wasn't exaggerating. I know he said he was a brujo in Mexico, and he was known in his village for his cures and spells, but how would my grandfather know our family went all the way back to Tenochtitlan?"

"Tenochtitlan?" Lori echoed.

"The floating city in Mexico. The one the Spanish invaded. It was the capital, bigger than most cities in Europe back then."

Her tired mind was struggling to keep up. What would this ancient city in Mexico have to do with Maria? "Julian, I'm sorry. I'm sorry I told Maria about all that, but I still don't understand why you think it's such a big deal. You're going to have to spell it out for me."

Julian sighed heavily. "All right. Maria's never had a history of her own, right? And then you told her about magic and brujos and how I can trace my family all the way back to ancient Mexico and the Aztecs. You heard her on the recordings. Suddenly, she's fascinated with that stuff. Who wouldn't be?

"And that ceremony last night? The pyramid? That's straight out of Tenochtitlan. And guess what else? The Aztecs used hallucinogenic mushrooms to talk to the gods too."

Lori stared up at the ceiling, clutching the arms of the camp chair. The mushroom images stared back at her.

"All of this is connected, Lori," Julian continued. "And what if my grandfather wasn't exaggerating? What if she did inherit some sort of gift? What if she's a bruja?"

He paused, slumping further down in his chair.

"Or what if she just believes it's true because she's taken so many mushrooms that it's messed with her head? And she's got a whole bunch of other people believing it too."

"So, what we saw wasn't an act?"

Julian's head slowly swiveled toward her, expression grim. "Maybe not."

From the far side of the room, Amy began to scream.

Chapter 39

Amy launched herself off the cot and scrabbled toward them on all fours, shrieking in terror.

The guards rushed in, looking around wildly, and Amy cried, "Over there," pointing at the cot.

Nearly dizzy with dread, Lori watched the two burly men gingerly lift the sleeping bags, look underneath, then toss them aside. The bald guy peered into the space between the cot and the wall, then beckoned his companion over. After exchanging amused glances, they began to laugh.

"Look who's not so brave now." Goatee Man smirked.

Amy pressed her face into Lori's knees, arms encircling her legs like a small child. Lori absently patted her back and watched Julian cross the room. He looked into the gap, then turned away with a scowl.

Lori gently pushed Amy away and hurried toward him. The men made no attempt to stop her. Julian was too busy trying to get himself under control to notice she'd moved.

Something was on the floor. Something long and furry and streaked with blood.

It was a deer skin, the head still attached.

Lori stepped away, a hand clamped over her mouth.

"Clean up on aisle five," Goatee Man sneered.

The guards hurried out of the room and returned moments later, carrying a box. They plucked the animal skin off the ground with gloved fingers and whisked it away.

"Things can be a little unpredictable around here," Goatee Man said before slamming the door shut behind them.

No one said anything for a long time.

When Amy finally turned her pale face to Lori and Julian, she asked, "Anyone care to guess what that was doing in here? Jesus. Are they sacrificing animals? What is *wrong* with these people?"

Even though the room was quiet, Lori sat and covered her ears, as if that could calm the thoughts swirling around in her head. Maria was no cult leader. She was too young. Not even thirty. Hadn't Erika always said Maria was highly sensitive, maybe even an empath? Someone else must have been responsible. Maria had to be under someone else's control. Someone older, someone evil.

"This isn't her," Lori cried. "She has Stockholm syndrome. She was kidnapped in the forest, and she's doing all this to survive."

Amy's eyes bulged. "Are you kidding me? Did she look like she wasn't in charge last night? What more evidence do you need?"

"Lori," Julian said in a warning voice from across the room.

"Lori what?" Lori stomped a foot. "That's easier to believe than all that other bullshit you've been talking about. Brujas. Aztecs. Ritual sacrifice. She was raised in Palo Alto, Julian. Went to summer camp at Stanford. She read up on ancient Mexico, so what? You think that's enough to turn her into a killer?"

Julian's mouth opened, then closed. He was staring past her, at the door.

Amy gave a little cry and shrank back. Lori spun around.

Maria was gliding into the room, wearing a long black sweater and jeans, long hair falling past her shoulders.

"Parents," she said, lifting her eyebrows.

Such a simple word, yet it ripped through Lori like a serrated knife. It held a lifetime of rebuke.

The calm demeanor Maria exuded contrasted with the whirlwind of emotions raging inside Lori. Seeing her adult daughter up close for the first time since Maria had gone missing brought back decades of regret. It clawed at her insides, reminding her of the day she'd given in to her father's demands and made the unbearable decision to give Maria up for adoption. Despite all the horrible things she'd witnessed, despite all her doubts about Maria, Lori felt a surge of love she hadn't expected and a fierce protectiveness toward this young woman who was still a stranger to her.

Lori stole a glance at Julian, his profile all hard angles, jaw working. What must he have been feeling, meeting his daughter after a lifetime of separation? A separation Lori had caused.

Julian seemed to have lost the ability to speak.

While Lori struggled to find her voice, Amy—seated on the floor with her back pressed against a wall—drummed her feet on the ground. "What the fuck is wrong with you?" she burst out, face twisted in fury.

"Nothing is wrong with me," Maria replied coldly. "You wouldn't understand."

Amy barked out a laugh. "Try me. I'm pretty sure there isn't a single thing you could say that would make me understand why you let everyone believe something horrible happened to you when you've been here all along, hiding, pretending to be a witch. Oh, *excuse* me. Pretending to be the *Spore Queen.*"

Lori stepped toward her daughter. "Maria, I don't understand. What's all this about? What's happening? When we started looking for you…" Her words trailed away.

Maria's eyes flicked to Julian. "I'm sorry. And I'm sorry about the deer skin. Our priest slept here last night. He shouldn't have left it behind. He's still learning." She hesitated. "We're all still learning."

"Learning what?" Lori cried. She wanted to run to Maria, hug her, shake her, get the truth out of her so she would know everything immediately.

Maria sighed. "The new ways. It's hard to explain. I wanted you to come. Both of you." She jerked her head in Amy's direction. "But not with her."

"Because you can't manipulate me like you can them," Amy said, rolling to her feet.

Maria's chin jutted out. "I don't need to manipulate anybody. They'll understand soon enough. We want them with us."

The word sent a chill up Lori's arms. "Who's *we?*"

"Me. And the one I follow."

In a few steps, Julian closed the gap separating him and his daughter. "Who is the one you follow, Maria?"

Lori watched, heart beating wildly, as Maria placed a hand on his shoulder.

"I think you can guess who it is, Dad." She paused. "Can I call you 'Dad,' or would you prefer Julian?"

Behind her, Amy muttered. "Oh please, spare me."

Maria swiveled her head toward Amy. "I can understand them trying to find me, Amy, but why are *you* here? You never liked me, did you? What are you doing here?"

Amy, back still pressed against the wall, looked away. "You left me your place in the will."

Maria gave a cold little laugh. "I forgot about that. You're here hoping to find proof that I'm dead. Well, I'm not. Too bad for you."

"Maria," Julian said, his voice tinged with disapproval.

If this family reunion—one Lori had fantasized about since giving up her child—wasn't such a nightmarish disaster, it would have been funny. After a lifetime of separation, Julian had stepped into the role of concerned father with shocking ease.

An amused smile came to Maria's lips. "Sorry, Dad." She winked. "But back to your question. I think you know who we all follow. In the old days, he might have been called 'Xipe Totec.'"

Julian reared his head back as if she'd slapped him. "No, no, no, Maria. It's not him. Is that why you're doing this?"

Obviously, Julian knew what Maria was talking about, but Lori didn't. Before the conversation continued in a direction she couldn't follow, she stepped between them. "What old days? Who is this man?"

Sweat glistened on Julian's forehead. "It's not a man," he said in a low voice. "It's one of the gods of ancient Mexico. The flayed god."

Maria's attention was fixed on Julian. She seemed to have forgotten Lori was in the room. "He represents the seasons and rebirth."

"Those guys last night…" Julian tipped his head back and moaned. "They were a sacrifice, then…?" The words died on his lips.

Maria looked away. "There are things we must do that can be hard to understand, but they are necessary."

"Like killing them with magic mushrooms?" Amy yelled. "What the hell is wrong with you!"

"Nothing at all." Maria coldly eyed her former friend.

Julian pointed a finger at Amy. "Can you please not talk?"

Amy's mouth opened, then closed. She flipped him off and spun around, facing the wall.

Julian's hands came up and gripped Maria's arms. "Your group worships Xipe Totec?"

The name sounded so strange to Lori, like *heap-ay-tow-tayck*.

"Of course," Maria replied. "I've seen him, and so have the others."

Julian scraped a hand through his hair. "Do you take mushrooms?"

"Of course I do. I was the first."

"What do you mean?"

"It's how all of this started. I came to the forest to do a story after a windstorm knocked down thousands of trees. But I discovered something beautiful. Amid all the destruction, there was so much activity. Fungus was growing everywhere. It was healing the forest. Digesting the deadwood and creating rich fertile soil for new saplings. I'd never seen anything like it. It felt like the forest was being reborn right in front of me.

"And then there was this mushroom, a beautiful and unusual one, and a voice was telling me to eat it. I didn't at first because I thought it might be dangerous. But the voice kept telling me it would be okay, so I tried it. It changed everything. It changed me. And it's going to change the world."

Maria was speaking in a low and steady voice. Earnest. Determined. The words chilled Lori's blood.

Julian continued. "How often do you take these mushrooms?"

"Every day." Maria patted his arm. "There's no reason to worry. It's safe. I know what I'm doing."

"Because Xipe Totec speaks to you? Tells you what to do?"

Maria gave a small laugh. "Not directly. But he has his way of communicating through the mushrooms and the rituals."

Julian bowed his head until his forehead touched Maria's shoulder. "Maria, I have something to ask you, mija, but you have to tell me the truth. No matter what, all right?"

Hearing the endearment, Maria's eyes glistened. "All right."

"When did the magic come to you?"

"After I first ate the mushroom."

"And you think it transformed you?"

"No. I *know* it did. Because I can do things I never could before."

"Like what?"

A long silence followed. Maria's eyebrows knit together, like she was trying to decide how much to reveal. "Sometimes, I can fly," she finally said, just loud enough for Lori to hear it.

A little cry escaped Lori's throat. Julian shot her a swift warning glance.

"Okay," he said. "So, you're a bruja, then? There's never been a woman who had the gift in our family, and no one's ever been able to fly. My grandfather always said if the family gift ever came to a woman, it would be powerful."

Maria nodded. "It is. I can feel it. It's like a fire in my veins."

Across the room, Amy snorted dismissively.

"Maria, I believe you have the magic, but listen to me. You don't know what's out there, talking to you. You think it's Xipe Totec because that's what you want to believe. It was in your mind already when you started taking the mushrooms. But you don't know what it really is. It could be something bigger and darker. You could have conjured some dark force, and it may be using your mind against you."

Maria was shaking her head. "No, no. I would know if that was happening. It's not. I would feel the evil. This feels good. And it's much bigger than me. It's not about me at all or getting rich or anything like that. This is something good. And important."

Lori had had enough. She stepped between them. "Why did you let us see the ceremony, Maria?"

Maria did a double take, startled Lori was standing so close. "Because you needed to see it. To believe. I want us to be together, but first, you need to believe."

"To believe our daughter is the leader of a cult?"

"It's not a cult." Maria's eyes narrowed, and she lifted her chin. "You were there. You saw him. You can't deny what your own eyes have seen."

"We didn't see anything because there wasn't anything to see!" Amy shouted.

Maria tilted her head to the side, turning questioning eyes on her father. "What does she mean? Of course you saw. He was there. In the sky. *Everyone* saw it."

Before Lori could reply, Julian shook his head. "No, we didn't. From where we were, we could only see you, on top of the pyramid."

Maria spun on her heel and began pacing in front of the door. "You had to have seen him!" she protested.

Lori wanted to give her a good shake. To snap her out of whatever kind of state she was in.

"Maria, what are your intentions now? You had your bodyguards bring us here. Are we your guests? Or your prisoners?"

Maria froze. Her hair lifted from her shoulders and floated away from her head. By the way Julian was staring, Lori knew she wasn't imagining it. Across the room, Amy gasped.

Then Maria turned toward Lori, her face a mask. "That's an interesting question," she said. "You have some decisions to make, parents. Let's see what you choose this time."

With that, she swept out of the room.

Debra Castaneda

Chapter 40

Ice in her veins, Amy stared at the door. Had she really seen Maria's hair float around her head with a life of its own, or had she imagined it?

Lori and Julian stood frozen, eyes wide with shock. Amy could practically see their thoughts darting around like frenzied bats in their heads, but she didn't care. She was outraged Julian had treated Maria as if she were normal and not mentally unstable or evil. Or both. At the same time, Amy was annoyed with Lori for having let Julian handle Maria, while she hovered in the background, fidgeting and wringing her hands.

Though, Amy had to give Maria credit. She could con her parents like Ferris Buehler. The way she'd looked at Julian with those big eyes and the way Julian had looked back at her—Maria playing the ultimate daddy's girl was enough to make Amy sick.

Lori turned away and faced the wall, obviously crying. Amy felt bad for her, but they had to do something. Her head throbbed where that idiot of a guard had clobbered her, and she needed medical attention. She probably had a concussion. For all Amy knew, she had a brain bleed and might be dead within hours.

The way Maria had glared at her sent shivers down her spine. Her friend's warm, welcoming eyes had become cold and piercing, as if she could see straight into Amy's soul.

Amy needed to make a plan to get the hell out of there. But she couldn't do it alone. With a sigh, she limped over to

Julian, who was looking past her with unseeing eyes. She needed to tone down her attitude.

"Listen, I know this must be hard for you," she began. "This isn't what you expected, and it must be devastating. But Maria said you have some decisions to make. I don't know about you, but that doesn't sound so good, considering what happened at the ceremony. We can't just sit around. We need to get out of here."

Amy paused and let her words sink in.

"Are you with me? Are we going to get the hell out of Dodge? Or do I need to make my own plan?"

Amy's heart pounded, her mouth going dry. The silence stretched on. When neither Julian nor Lori answered, she repeated her question with more urgency.

"I said, are you with me, or am I leaving on my own?"

Lori spun around, eyes red, face streaked with tears. "Would you give me some space?"

Amy flinched and stepped back. "I'm sorry, Lori, but it's not like we have all the time in the world to process our feelings. Shit is happening."

The door banged open, and Amy jumped, realizing her mistake. Guards had been right outside. They had probably heard every word.

Paunchy Guy stood in the doorway, glaring at Amy. A moment later, Knife Guy and Goatee Man strode into the room, grabbed her arms, fingers pressing into her skin, and pulled her toward the door. She was taller than both, but Amy was no match for their bulk, determination, and strength.

With mounting desperation, she let herself go limp, dragging the tips of her boots on the ground to slow their progress. The men suddenly released her arms, and Amy pitched forward, chin striking the ground. Her head bounced, and she tasted blood in her mouth.

Somewhere behind her, Lori screamed, "Amy!"

"Motherfuckers," Amy snarled, trying to push herself into a standing position.

Hands roughly gripped her elbows and propelled her out of the kiln's dim interior into the daylight. People milling about the campsite stopped to stare. Amy recognized one of them. The mushroom expert—Maria's boyfriend, or whatever he was.

"Gabriele!" she cried.

He was standing next to an older man wearing an expensive-looking jacket. And there was someone else too. A tall, thin young man with sharp features—Karl Ackerman, the techie who'd gone missing in Nils Forest. All three stared back, their expressions unreadable.

Gabriele whispered something into the older man's ear, and he gave a slight nod, then looked down at the open notebook in his hands.

What the hell was going on?

Amy had suspected Gabriele knew more than he was telling when she interviewed him at his farm. But if he was here, he was deeply involved, and how could that be? The man was smart, probably brilliant. He had a Ph.D., had published books about mycology, and taught classes at the local college. Gabriele had too much sense to get involved with a cult. Especially one led by a crazy woman who terrified people into believing she was a powerful witch, or whatever Maria was supposed to be.

Amy continued to call to Gabriele, her voice shrill with desperation, but she was quickly dragged toward a stone hut at the edge of the clearing. A door opened, and she was shoved inside, sprawling.

"You can holler all you like in here," a voice barked.

The door slammed behind her, and a latch fell into place.

Chapter 41

Amy rolled onto her side, breathing hard. The room was small and empty. Walls made of stone. An earthen floor. A door too thick to kick down, and even if she tried, someone would see her, and the guards would return. There was probably one standing outside. With a cry of frustration, she kicked the door anyway.

Light streamed in from a gap between the top of the stone walls and the roof made of moss-covered wooden slats. If she had something to stand on, she might be able to push on the part of the ceiling closest to the forest to see if she could climb through and drop down into the trees. But there was nothing.

Amy guessed the hut must have been used for storage when the kilns were still operating.

There was nothing else to do but sit and ponder her predicament. Amy was trapped and alone. Her body had taken a beating, and there wasn't a part of her not aching, burning, or stinging.

She'd managed to alienate Lori and Julian. Amy would have put money on the father as the more sensible of the two, but she'd seen the way Julian looked at his daughter. Yet another man who had fallen under Maria's spell. Maybe Julian was right. Maybe Maria was a witch after all. Then Amy laughed, this time at her own foolishness for even entertaining such a thought.

Cold stones pressing into her back, chin resting on her knees, Amy quickly lost track of time. No one came to check on her, offer her water, or bring her food. At least she didn't have to go to the bathroom yet. She stared into the darkness, her mind going blank.

After what felt like hours, a low hum rumbled through the ground, jolting her out of her stupor. She sat up, dazed, her eyes instinctively darting toward the door. But it remained shut, offering no clues as to the source of the disturbance.

The walls began to vibrate. Amy scrambled to her feet, the humming sound growing louder and more urgent. She frantically searched for the source of the noise. On the other side of the cramped room, the ground near the wall was shifting and rising, chunks of soil loosening. A hole had begun to form.

What the fuck?

Her mouth went dry. Pulse racing, she stumbled backward until she hit the wall.

At the center of the hole in the ground, mushrooms sprouted. Bright and beautiful in vibrant shades of orange and purple. The mushrooms grew in a ring surrounded by what seemed to be a crown of twigs covered in moss. Under it was a tangle of hair and finally a face. Clumps of dirt slid off, revealing its owner. It was Maria, dark eyes glittering, mouth twisted in a sardonic smile.

Amy let out a piercing scream and covered her eyes with shaking hands. The low rumbling continued.

Hands took her own and gently pulled them away from her face. Amy reared her head back and collided with the unforgiving stone wall. A trickle of blood ran down her scalp.

Warm breath caressed her face, and Amy let out another shriek. When her eyes flicked open, she saw Maria wearing a crown made of mushrooms, dressed in a flowing purple gown.

Maria broke the silence. "Now do you believe?"

Her shock faded, and anger started to resurface. Amy looked past Maria and her smug smile of triumph. The humming had stopped, but the evidence of Maria's emergence from the ground was still there—a pile of dirt and a gaping hole.

Amy'd been taken to this pathetic excuse for a jail cell for a reason, and she was beginning to suspect what that was. What if this was where the cult sent its disbelievers? And what if what she'd just seen was more stagecraft, something straight out of an illusionist's playbook?

Amy straightened her shoulders and forced herself to return Maria's gaze.

"Do I believe what? That you're some kind of witch? The Spore Queen? Yeah right. You can tell yourself that all you want. You fucked your way into getting Gabriele Bruno to believe you too, but to me, you're nothing but a fake. A killer fake. But just a fake."

Maria stepped back, stung. "Can we get over this, Amy? I know I wasn't your favorite person in the world, but we were friends. Or at least, I thought we were. And you're brilliant. I can use your help. We can *all* use your help."

Maria's sudden shift in tone caught Amy off guard. The familiar warmth had returned, and with it, Maria's pleading eyes.

Maybe there was a way out of this. If she played along, she might survive long enough to figure out a way to escape. "What did you have in mind?"

Maria placed her hand on Amy's arm, causing a slight electric sensation to course through her body. Startled, Amy quickly pulled away. She must have imagined it, or maybe it was just a bit of static electricity passing between them.

The mushrooms atop Maria's crown swayed, as if moved by a gentle breeze. Maria said nothing but continued to gaze at Amy with intense dark eyes shining with an unnatural glow. Then she reached up and plucked a mushroom from her crown. She cupped it in both hands and held it out to Amy.

"Take this. Take it and join me here. When you learn of the work we're doing, you'll be excited to be part of the movement."

Amy stared at the mushroom. It was time she admitted the truth, if only to herself. Maria did seem to possess some supernatural powers, and Julian—a reasonable man—seemed convinced his daughter was a bruja. Plus there was no denying Maria had an organized network of followers who were willing to do whatever she wanted, no matter how crazy.

Amy's resentment had led her to treat Maria with a complete lack of respect. Which was like stepping into a cage with a hungry tiger, not fully realizing the danger of its sharp teeth and claws. And Maria didn't deserve it.

Amy looked around the room at the swaying mushrooms. There was no explaining that strange, unsettling movement. With a shiver, she shifted her attention back to Maria and gently pushed Maria's hands away.

"Whatever you've got going on here, Maria, I don't think it's for me." Amy gave a little laugh and shrugged. "You know me. I'm a city girl. I couldn't even handle that Eco Warrior club you wanted me to join, and that was just one meeting a week and a few cleanups in the canyons."

Maria met her gaze, expression softening. "Then I'm sorry. If you don't want to take the mushroom, it's decided for me. There's nothing I can do."

Goosebumps prickled across Amy's skin like a thousand tiny needles. The air suddenly felt oppressive, thick with tension and uncertainty. The weight of her situation crushed down on Amy, like sandbags sitting on her shoulders.

"What's that supposed to mean? *It's decided?*"

The warmth drained from Maria's eyes. "I mean, it's out of my control. Those who refuse the mushroom must meet their fate."

"Like those guys last night?" The image of the young men thrashing around, then falling to the ground, lifeless, flashed in Amy's mind. But it was all part of the show. All part of the cult's sadistic brainwashing.

Maria sighed. "They ate the mushroom, but they were not believers in their hearts, and they were not transformed. Those whom the fungus rejects are sacrificed to Xipe Totec. It is the way."

Amy's heart sank. This wasn't working. She'd relied on Maria's good nature to let her out of this situation, but Maria wasn't the same person anymore. "You're going to sacrifice me? Are you fucking kidding?" Her voice was loud and shrill.

Maria shrugged, her expression blank.

There was no reasoning with her. Maria was a self-proclaimed bruja and the leader of a cult, but there was no way Amy was going to allow herself to be sacrificed. Taking the damn mushroom was no guarantee either. She still might end up dead.

Maria had come up out of that hole in the ground. It had to lead somewhere. Busting out of the door wasn't an option. Amy's only way out was the way Maria had come in.

They were standing too close. Maria was less than two feet away, and Amy needed room to maneuver.

Amy made a big show of wincing and rubbing her backside. "Pretty sure I'm going to be black and blue after all that manhandling," she said, stepping away.

She shifted her body to avoid making eye contact with Maria for what came next.

Amy tensed her muscles, lowered her head, and channeled all her strength. Then she rammed into Maria with the full force of her body. Maria stumbled backward, her head hitting the unforgiving stone wall with a sickening thud.

Amy's heart pounded, and she lunged toward the spot where Maria had emerged from the ground. But clods of dirt tumbled back down into the hole, forcing her to fall on her knees in a frantic attempt to scoop out the falling debris and keep the hole open. Amy gritted her teeth, fingers becoming raw. She clawed at the soil, fighting against the relentless flow of earth pouring in—panic rising as her only means of escape disappeared.

A sound behind her stopped her futile efforts. Amy turned to look over her shoulder. Maria was struggling to stand, one hand holding the back of her head. Her eyes seemed to glitter in the dim light. Instead of looking at Amy, she fixed her gaze on the wall beside her. Maria lifted a hand and flicked her fingers, lips moving silently.

A soft, unfamiliar sound filled the room—a strange susurration seemingly coming from behind the stone wall. Amy watched, eyes blinking, as a white object squeezed through a crack between the smooth rocks. It unfolded and stretched until it resembled a large round cushion. But it wasn't a cushion. It was a giant mushroom.

Amy couldn't look away, mesmerized by the fungus's sudden appearance. After a moment, she tore her gaze away and turned back to Maria, who let out a raspy chuckle. Then she pursed her lips and blew at the massive growth.

The giant mushroom exploded, releasing a cloud of white dust.

Amy coughed. The room spun. She felt dizzy and slightly nauseous. And then she could feel nothing at all as the ground came rushing up to meet her.

Chapter 42

When she awoke, Amy heard voices.

Her mouth was dry, and her body ached.

She heard a man's voice, then cheering.

Amy was still dazed from the effects of the spores, but she immediately recognized the voice. It belonged to Gabriele Bruno.

She heard more voices outside the door, people walking by, talking excitedly about sacrifices and bloodletting.

Man, this was a dark group.

Amy squinted at the small opening near the ceiling. The light was fading.

The smell of woodsmoke filled the room, causing her to cough and cover her mouth. The aroma of roasting meat soon followed. The back of her throat protested—still uncomfortably queasy from the spores. When had she last eaten? Not since she'd arrived at this camp of nightmares. And still, no one had come to check on her or offer her food.

Where were Julian and Lori? Were they out there now, mingling with Maria's followers, maybe hanging out with their daughter in the private room behind the kiln? Either way, they could go fuck themselves.

As evening descended, the temperature dropped, causing Amy to shiver in her jacket. How long did they plan to keep her locked up? When her bladder protested, she banged on the door for help, but no one responded. Eventually, with no other options, she relieved herself in a corner of the room. The indignity of squatting and urinating onto a dirt floor brought tears.

Amy still didn't think Maria Hart was a witch, despite having seen her conjure a mushroom from thin air, then making it explode with spores. Spores that sent Amy into a deep sleep much like death.

That shove should have knocked Maria out or dazed her at least. There wasn't a trace of blood on the wall where Maria had hit her head, but Amy remembered the sound of Maria smacking against the stones. There should have been blood everywhere.

Maria had asked for her help. Refusing, just hours before another ceremony, had been an idiotic move. The ceremony. This time, Amy wouldn't be allowed to just watch. She'd be a participant.

The thought suddenly made everything feel real. No. No. No. It wasn't real. It was all a sham. *It had to be.* And yet, she was shaking uncontrollably. Every noise outside made her flinch. She'd broken out in a cold sweat.

Maybe the station had tried to call her cell phone. If she was lucky, maybe somebody would freak out when she failed to answer. Amy could only hope they'd alerted the police. Maybe there were people out there now, searching for her in the forest.

But even if they were, Maria and her magical fungus would prevent them from getting too close, just as she'd done with the previous search teams.

Fuck. She actually believed Maria had magical powers.

Amy collapsed on the ground, covering her face with an arm. A moan of desperation left her throat.

Escape was unlikely. Even if she somehow managed it, Amy was a city girl in the middle of a huge forest, and she wouldn't get far before falling down another hill and breaking her neck.

Someone outside began to play a guitar. There was laughter and singing, mostly songs from the seventies. What the hell was going on? They sounded high. Of course, they did. It was magic mushroom time. Maria was probably off somewhere with Gabriele, fucking their brains out. Isn't that what people in cults did?

Maybe that's what would happen next—people pairing off and sneaking away to their tents for a screwfest before tonight's main event.

Amy leaned against the wall, nervously chewing on her lip while the merriment continued outside. The longer she listened, the more unsettling it became.

Eventually, the cheerful singing was replaced by a haunting chant that made her skin crawl.

Still weak from the effects of the spores, Amy waited. The chanting voices faded away but were soon replaced by the familiar voices of her captors.

The door creaked open. Light flooded into the room, revealing lanterns held by towering figures. The guards had returned.

"Don't make a scene," one of them warned.

By that time, Amy was too exhausted and overwhelmed by fear to struggle. All her courage and determination had faded away, and she let herself be taken by the two men, blinking when the torch light hit her eyes. Outside, the tables and food had been cleared away, and people milled around the base of the pyramid.

Amy was only half aware of the blurred, staring faces whispering together as she passed. She was being half carried, half dragged up the pyramid by the men, their arms fully supporting her weight.

Maria waited atop the platform. Standing beside her was the tall, slender man wearing the deer mask. Up close, it was hideous. A stitched-together thing made of real fur. Maria was still clad in her long purple dress, which showed no signs of its journey through the ground.

Lori and Julia were there too, huddled together, holding hands. Julian watched Amy approach with wide and frightened eyes. Lori's face was swollen and red, like she'd been crying for hours. Maria bent down to pick a pale mushroom from the side of the pyramid.

Amy nearly hyperventilated with anxiety, watching Maria crush the mushroom on a grinding stone sitting atop the table. When Maria turned to face her, she held out a spoon, a small smile on her lips.

Julian spoke softly. "Maria, no."

Maria ignored him, her dark eyes locking onto Amy, glittering with challenge. Amy was too numb and weak to resist. Swaying slightly, she struggled to keep her balance. Suddenly, she wanted nothing more than to crawl under the table and escape into sleep. Maybe when she woke up, the nightmare would be over.

Maria stepped closer, holding the spoon to Amy's lips and forcing them apart. Amy could swat the spoon away, knock it out of Maria's hand. But that would only prolong the inevitable. With a tremulous sigh, Amy opened her mouth and tasted the spongy, fibrous mushroom—an earthy sweetness similar to sunflower seeds. She swallowed it down, and then the guards were guiding her to a pillow. Maria settled in beside her, legs crossed, expression untroubled.

Amy was grateful she couldn't see the people below. Julian and Lori receded from sight, her vision beginning to tunnel. It became just the two of them: Amy, with her matted hair and filthy clothes, and Maria, adorned with an elaborate headpiece made of flowers and mushrooms swaying gently in the breeze.

A few times, Amy felt herself leaning to the side, in danger of toppling over, but firm hands kept her steady.

Maria's locks floated around her head when she lifted off her pillow, several inches into the air. She raised her arms into the sky, and a crack of thunder echoed through the atmosphere. Amy clapped her hands over her ears, but her fingers were no match against the awful noise. The platform beneath them vibrated.

Amy looked up at the dark sky. A fissure was forming, revealing a blinding white light tearing it apart, wider and wider. A craggy face emerged. Giant hands were pulling apart the opening as if trying to give birth to itself.

A burst of energy surged between Maria and the monster in the sky. An inhuman howl ripped through the air, its outrage directed at Amy.

And she could feel its anger. Anger at how she had treated Maria. Anger that she was jealous of the woman who had shown her kindness. Anger she'd never seen Maria for who she truly was—a woman relinquished by her mother and raised with an emotional wound that would never heal.

And Amy had done her insidious best to make it worse.

She had doubted Maria. Mocked her. And now, she would face the consequences.

Amy'd eaten the mushroom Maria and the sky monster had conjured. The fungus knew what was in her heart and head, and both were filled with envy and betrayal.

In a split second, she registered the terrifying appearance of the being looming above, but she also sensed its true intentions, which were far from what Amy had expected. Its intentions were…good.

With that realization came the knowledge she'd been wrong. Wrong be so cruel to Maria, wrong to deny that something beyond her understanding was at work. Wrong to assume the cult was dangerous.

She could see clearly how wrong she'd been, and she let out a desperate cry of despair.

"Wait," Amy pleaded. "I understand now! I can help, I swear it!"

But it was too late. Trails of white fungal threads were snaking toward her. Within seconds, they'd wrapped around her feet and slithered up her legs. Time seemed to slow, and she frantically struggled against the bindings, but the more she fought against them, the tighter they constricted. Heart pounding in sheer terror, Amy clawed at the filaments. She couldn't feel her legs.

"Maria, please!" she screamed. But the threads were already winding around her middle, squeezing the air from her lungs. After a final gasp, Amy's vision began to blur. And then, all was darkness.

Chapter 43

Lori sat up with a gasp. The last thing she remembered was sitting on top of the pyramid, swallowing the mushroom Maria had offered them. The heavens had broken open, but she'd still seen nothing in the sky.

And somehow, she'd ended up in a sleeping bag in the back room of the kiln, still dressed in her clothes. Julian was next to her, his face turned toward the wall. Wood smoke drifted in, the sharp tang stinging her nose and making her eyes water.

Without waking Julian, she got up and went over to the door. It wasn't locked. Cautiously, Lori opened it and peered outside, expecting someone to come charging in her direction. But no one came. The main room was empty, all the furniture gone. The door to the outside was ajar. There was no one to stop her, so she pushed it open and stepped into a beautiful, crisp morning. In the distance, birds chirped in the trees.

The clearing in front of the kilns was a bustle of activity. The pyramid was gone, and men were throwing wood onto a large fire on the other side. They must have dismantled the pyramid, Lori thought, and they were burning the evidence.

Half the tents were already gone, the rest in the process of being taken down. Amidst the chaos, there were shouts and calls while people packed up their belongings. There were plastic bins everywhere. Teams of two were carting them off into the forest.

A hand touched her arm, and she spun around, pulse racing.

It was Julian. "Are they leaving?" His voice was hoarse.

Maria appeared around the kiln. "We're leaving." She smiled brightly and handed them two mugs.

Lori accepted hers and eyed the brown liquid with suspicion.

Maria cleared her throat. "It's just coffee."

Lori's hands shook, and she regarded her daughter. How could she look so calm, so composed, after what had happened to Amy?

"I don't understand!" she cried, voice shaking. "You were roommates. You were in college together. She wasn't always nice, Maria, but she hardly deserved to die!" She couldn't rid herself of the image, the way those white threads had emerged from the mushrooms and covered Amy, seeming to swallow her whole.

Maria let out a heavy sigh, eyebrows drawing together. "Who said she's dead? She should never have come here. I'm sorry, but it was out of my control."

Lori allowed herself a moment of hope. "Is Amy alive?"

Instead of replying, Maria shrugged.

"If you're a bruja, you should have been able to do something to save her." Lori put a shaky hand to her head. She was exhausted, and every nerve seemed to jangle.

"It doesn't always work like that." Maria's voice was tinged with regret. "I'm actually sorry it happened, but there was nothing I could have done to prevent it."

Lori's throat felt like it was closing up. She had to drink some coffee to get the words out. "I still don't understand, Maria. Any of it. What is all this? What the hell are you doing?"

Lori stole a glance at Julian, trying to read his thoughts. But he was in his own world, not paying attention to their conversation. His eyes were unfocused and glassy, surveying the remains of the camp.

Maria suddenly seemed to register his condition. She placed her hand on his arm, then hurried away and returned with two camp chairs, motioning for them to have a seat. Maria grabbed another chair and positioned it in front of them.

She cleared her throat as she sat down. "You passed the test. I wasn't sure you would. I wasn't sure you'd even take the mushrooms. But you did. Thank you." She hesitated, knee bouncing. "That means you can come with us now."

"To do what?" Lori replied coldly. "Kill more people?"

Maria sat back, stung.

Julian reached out and squeezed Lori's arm. She shook him off.

"Maria, I'm not done talking about this. A bunch of fungus smothered your former roommate, and those two kids the other night looked like they were poisoned. What the hell is going on? What is this about?" She was practically screaming now.

Maria stared down at her lap and said nothing, her tangled hair falling over her face.

Julian leaned forward and addressed his daughter through clenched teeth. "Maria. You can't avoid this. Not if you want us to go anywhere with you. We deserve an explanation."

When Maria raised her head, she looked around, biting her lip.

Julian tapped her knee, reminding her they were still there, waiting. "Let's have it, Maria."

Maria slumped back in her chair and drew up her knees as if trying to make herself as small as possible. Lori sensed she was stalling for time, trying to figure out how much to reveal. Her eyes darted back and forth before finally settling on Julian.

With a deep breath, she seemed to come to a decision. "All right. I've already told you about who he is but not what he wants. And that's the most important thing."

"And what does he want?" Julian prompted.

Lori wondered at his patience. With every fiber in her being, she wanted to jump up and shake some sense into Maria. But she forced herself to stay still and silent. Julian connected with Maria better than she did, at least for now.

Maria surprised Lori by smiling. She straightened in her chair, shoulders back. "It's simple, really. Mushrooms can help save the world. But they can't do it alone. That's why he has returned, to find someone like me to get things started. I didn't completely understand it at first, but when I told Gabriele about my visions, he believed me. And when I showed him the mushroom that appeared in my visions, he tested it, and he was so excited. He got it right away."

Maria became more animated, talking faster and waving her hands.

"Gabriele says he's never seen this species before. It's different. It grows amazingly quickly and can break down all sorts of material in almost no time at all. The only problem is, they can take a long, long time to spread. We don't have that kind of time.

"But humans are awesome at transportation. We've spread products, ideas, and viruses all over the globe, so why can't we spread spores?

"Well, I think we can. I'm creating a human-fungal network that can begin to repair the damage we've done to the world, and we're starting with the forests. Our people will travel the world, bringing spores to areas that need help. And you'll come with us! You'll be a part of it!"

Lori went completely still. Whatever she'd been expecting, it wasn't an invitation. Maria made it sound scientific and perfectly reasonable. But there was something else. Maria had made it sound like an offer they couldn't refuse. Lori and Julian exchanged a brief wary glance.

With glowing eyes, Maria leaned forward. "I know it's a lot to ask. But please. Please come."

Lori gripped the arms of her chair, lightheaded, and continued to stare at Maria. The idea of leaving everything behind to join a mysterious fungal team, or cult, or whatever, was beyond anything she could comprehend. Plus, there was something in Maria's expression, just under the surface. Lori couldn't quite make it out. A flicker of uncertainty? Or maybe it was fear?

Finally, the words erupted from her throat. "This network, or whatever it is…It doesn't sound cheap. Will your god provide the cash? If you think your grandparents will bankroll this, you're mistaken. They've supported you all your life. I made sure of it. It was what they owed you, but this will never, ever happen if you're expecting them to pay for it."

As soon as the words left her mouth, Lori regretted them. She'd spoken to Maria in the same hateful way her father often spoke to her. How could she expect to forge a relationship with her daughter when she behaved like such a bitch?

Maria shook her head. "I appreciate everything they have done, honestly. But I don't need their money. We already have the funding."

Lori couldn't believe her casual nonchalance.

"How do you have funding?" No traditional bank would make a loan for such a crazy plan. Perhaps Maria's mycologist boyfriend had money. Or maybe some of the members of the cult—for that's what it was, no matter what Maria said—were not only gullible, but wealthy.

"Money is the least of our worries." Maria smiled. "With a tent and a plane ticket, we can do a tremendous amount of good."

Lori asked her to explain, but Maria simply shrugged.

"What if we refuse?" Julian asked. "We both have lives. Your mother has a job in the city. I have a farm. And we may have other ideas about the future…"

Lori turned and looked at Julian, but he avoided her gaze.

Maria looked at Julian, then at Lori, and grinned. "You mean you're getting together? That would be amazing! You can just—I don't know—take some time off and come with us. To help. I don't want to do this alone."

"What about Gabriele?" Lori said. "Won't he be there for you?" The words sounded accusatory, even to Lori's ears.

Maria nodded. "Of course he'll be there, but he's not my parents and…" Her words drifted off. She didn't need to say the rest. *You owe me.*

Julian reached over and took Maria's hands in his. Maria gazed into his eyes as if transfixed.

"And what?"

"Sometimes, I'm a little afraid," she whispered, glancing up at the sky.

Julian looked up too, a cloud passing over his face. "Do you still believe it's Xipe Totec up there?"

"Yes. I hope so." Maria lifted her chin. "Whatever it is, it knows what it's doing."

"Including ritual sacrifice." Julian's voice dripped with bitterness.

"The old ways die hard," she whispered, staring into her lap. "But once we prove ourselves, things may change."

Julian still gripped his daughter's hands. "I already said this once before, Maria, but it's something I'd like you to think

228

about. Please. These mushrooms you're taking are powerful. You already had all that Aztec history in your head. You could be seeing what you want to see."

"But other people see him too," Maria replied, voice rising.

"Because you told them what to expect. It's like a mass hallucination."

Maria's mouth opened, then closed. In one fluid movement, she stood. "That's not what's happening," she said stiffly. "I'm sorry you don't believe me, but I still hope you come with us." She hurried away toward the last remaining tent.

Julian's words were like cold hands squeezing Lori's neck. Her scalp prickled, and she shivered. "Julian, I think you went too far. She's in over her head. She needs our help."

Julian nodded. His eyes flickered past her, toward the fire still burning across the clearing.

Maria might have been the Spore Queen, but there was no way Lori was going to let her daughter begin this strange new chapter in her life without at least one parent to support her.

"We need to do this, Julian."

Despite the chilly mountain air, sweat beaded on his forehead. He reached for her hand and gave it a squeeze. "Yeah. That's what I'm thinking too."

Chapter 44

With hands on hips, David Eager surveyed his former retreat center, now officially closed for business. Closed for the hospitality business anyway.

He stood in the middle of the meadow, taking it all in.

The new facility didn't have a name. It didn't need one. It was merely a convenient place for everyone to gather privately until the next phase of their venture. They didn't have a lot of time, so he'd ordered modular prefab cabins and a two-story shipping container with glass windows to serve as a classroom. Gabriele Bruno would use it to teach the team members how to cultivate the fungus before they set out on their assignments.

At first, David had been apprehensive about the quality of the recruits, as he preferred to call them. Some were rough around the edges, and their behavior in the forest had been less than ideal. But after regularly ingesting a custom mushroom mixture prepared by Gabriele, they calmed down. The wild sex, partying, and the occasional violence of the early days had stopped, and a sense of discipline and purpose had emerged.

They were embarking on a complicated endeavor, but not once had David questioned whether they would be successful.

He had all the proof he needed. He *was* all the proof he needed.

The spores had cured his Lewy body dementia. That was something unknown to medical science. His doctors could not explain it, and when he tried, they could not believe it.

After taking in his miraculous recovery, Maria's mother had approached him numerous times, peppering him with questions. Sometimes, he'd catch her gazing nervously at the surrounding forest or the vast expanse of sky above.

His illness seemed like a fevered dream now, and each recruit had their own story. They all knew they'd been forever changed by the fungus and were about to take on a monumental task. It would be an enormous amount of work, but if he could be healed, so could the planet. David would do whatever it took to see it through.

The front door to his house opened, and Lori emerged alone. He'd assigned Maria's parents the largest cabin, so she must have been visiting her daughter. It was nice to see them spending more time together.

At his invitation, Maria and Gabriele had moved into his second-floor bedroom for some much-needed privacy. Maria especially appreciated the set of double doors on the upper deck that allowed her to exit whenever she grew restless, which was happening more frequently since they'd left the forest. She was anxious to move onto the next phase of their venture.

When Lori looked his way, he waved. She hurried over to him, dodging workmen and supplies scattered across the meadow. Concern was etched on her face, lines deepening with the passing of each uncertain day.

"I've been thinking," she said without preamble, "about the fungus curing you. Gabriele says fungus can do all sorts of amazing things, and it's possible these are even sentient. What if the fungus is just trying to manipulate you? What if it just wants your wealth?"

David threw his head back and laughed. "Well then, it's welcome to it. My money wasn't doing anything important anyway. And if it's some kind of trick, then it can trick me some more because I've never felt better in my life."

"But what if the cure is just for you?" Lori persisted. "What if it doesn't work for anyone else?"

The corners of David's mouth stretched into a wide grin. "I have a medical startup that is studying that exact thing. Gabriele is working with them to identify some promising treatments for frontal lobe dementias."

Lori shot him an incredulous look. "You're kidding? You're already funding all of this." She gestured toward the ongoing construction.

"And other projects too." He couldn't keep the pride from his voice.

"Just how much money *do* you have?"

David gave another booming laugh. "Plenty."

David had to hand it to the chefs. They'd done an excellent job preparing dinner for the group, their first official post-forest meal together. Roast beef and chicken, twice-baked potatoes, green beans topped with fried shallots. Chocolate cake and apple crumble for dessert. Comfort food. That's what they'd needed. And endless glasses of local wine. David enjoyed his pinot noir. He was no longer worried about alcohol counteracting his medications—he'd thrown them all away.

Not everyone had been able to make it. Some members had stayed in their rooms, still recovering from their time in the woods. Maria and Gabriele sat apart from the others in the dining room, at a table for two in a dark corner lit only by a candle.

In the forest, as Maria's power grew, she'd stayed in her room behind the kiln and only appeared at night for ceremonies, cementing her status as Spore Queen. Now, her relationship to her followers was evolving to be one of persuasion with subtlety and finesse.

It was her job to transform a religion into a business.

Gabriele was her confidant and ally in this delicate, difficult dance. David sipped his wine and observed Maria and Gabriele engaged in a hushed conversation. He couldn't make out the words over the laughter and clinking of glasses filling the hall, but he guessed Gabriele was still trying to convince Maria to give a speech. She'd always insisted it was David's job to communicate their mission, but Gabriele believed people wanted to hear from her too.

Gabriele had already spoken to the group about the extraordinary power of the new mushrooms Maria had discovered in Nils Forest. The mycologist was a gifted speaker, and he'd saved the best for last.

"I am now sure this new species of fungus is sentient. There is evidence it can communicate directly with the Spore Queen, which is something David has long suspected. I look forward to discovering more about its capabilities."

David knew there was much more to learn. He even thought it possible the fungus was behind Maria's visions of the god in the sky, but he thought it best to keep that theory to himself.

Rising from his chair at the head of the table, David stood in front of the bank of windows with their view of the forest. Lori and Julian exchanged a quick look, expressions guarded. Maria's parents still had some reservations, but David was confident they would eventually come around.

"Good evening, everyone," he began.

The room fell silent, and all eyes turned to him. He cleared his throat and pushed up the sleeves of his turtleneck sweater, exuding the confidence that came with his successful Silicon Valley pedigree.

"On behalf of myself and our Spore Queen, we'd like to thank you all for joining us. Not just for being here tonight, but for those critical moments in Nils Forest when we came together as strangers, thrown together by circumstance but knowing that each of us has been selected to be a part of something extraordinary. Something revolutionary. Tonight, we're here to mark the beginning of a journey like no other. A journey that has the potential to change the world."

David paused, allowing his words to sink in. The flickering candlelight cast dancing shadows on the faces in the audience. Eyes gleamed with anticipation.

"As many of you may know, I was battling Lewy body dementia when I first met Maria Hart. I could barely walk, couldn't sleep, and suffered from debilitating hallucinations. But after she came to the forest and brought forth a new fungus, she opened a portal to limitless possibilities. And to hope. I am living proof of its remarkable potential. If this species of fungi has the ability to cure me, it holds within it the key to healing our planet and ourselves."

David continued, his voice steady and resolute.

"For too long, the world has borne the weight of thoughtless human ambition and greed. It has suffered enormously from the consequences of our actions. But tonight, I stand before you to tell you that there is hope. We are no longer alone. Maria Hart has been chosen to lead us, to travel the world, guided by the unfathomable power of the new fungus. She's already proved that she can command the mushrooms at will, and they will obey. Under her direction, the fungus has neutralized threats, been medicine for some, and brought about a miraculous cure for myself, and the things she will do next will astonish the globe."

A murmur of excitement rippled through the crowd when Maria stood, acknowledging her followers with a solemn nod. Behind her, a golden trumpet mushroom sprouted from the wall.

Warmth spread through his body, and David continued. "We have gathered here as part of a new collective, united by a common purpose, driven by a shared belief there is a higher power at work that will transform the planet for the better and that it's our destiny to see it through."

David took a moment to scan their faces for any signs of hesitation but saw nothing but unwavering devotion in their eyes.

"There is no time to waste. Beginning tomorrow, we will operate on a twenty-four-seven basis, with the goal of understanding the true potential of this new species of fungi. Our resident mycologist, Gabriel Bruno, will be leading the instruction. So tonight, we celebrate. In the morning, we begin an exciting new phase that will culminate in assignments that will take us around the world."

Cheers and applause erupted in the room. David sat down, basking in the shared sense of purpose crackling in the room like a field of energy. It was a feeling he'd experienced many times before, but this time, it promised more than a new gadget or clever new bit of software.

He glanced at Maria. She gave him a little wave and smiled.

David smiled back. But for all her power, he did not envy her.

Chapter 45

Since Lori had reunited with Maria, she couldn't stop worrying about her daughter.

Maria moved around the compound with a near manic energy, spending most of her time in the mushroom grow house with the fungus, sporting dark circles beneath her eyes.

"She shouldn't be taking that damn stuff," Lori said to Julian over breakfast, before they went their separate ways.

"Gabriele says she's taking micro doses," Julian replied. "Nothing to worry about."

Lori shook her head. "But you've seen her. She doesn't look right."

"No," Julian admitted. "But what can he do? She's in uncharted medical waters."

Like Lori and Julian, Gabriele had become concerned about the amount of mushrooms Maria had been consuming. He attempted to taper Maria's dosage, as he had successfully done with most of the other members of the group, but her body reacted violently to the change. She'd had a seizure and felt ill for several days.

Lori had suggested they take Maria to a hospital so they could oversee her withdrawal, but Gabriele and David agreed doctors lacked the knowledge to deal with her. They feared she'd be treated like an addict who needed to get clean as opposed to a bruja who had a complex, intertwined relationship with the fungus.

In the end, they persuaded Lori the mushrooms were unlikely to harm their host, that they really had no choice but to trust that Maria and the fungus would arrive at an equilibrium of some sort.

But Lori feared traveling long distances under difficult circumstances would prove to be too much for Maria if she became too frail. Yet she had no choice but to trust in Gabriele. He was, after all, the mushroom expert, and it was obvious he loved her daughter.

One night, at dinner with Maria and Gabriele, Julian pulled out something from his jacket pocket and set it on the table. It was the small black and white photo of his grandfather taken in a garden somewhere in rural Mexico. The woman who looked exactly like Maria was there in her frilly dress, staring back at them.

Gabriele leaned over and studied the picture. A moment later, he said, "Wow. When was this taken?" Without waiting for a reply, he turned to Maria. "You're a dead ringer for this lady. Is this your grandmother, Julian?"

Never taking his eyes from Maria's face, Julian said, "No. I have no idea who she is because she's never been in the picture before, and it's been in my family for as long as I can remember."

Maria's gaze remained fixed on the photo, lips twitching.

"You're kidding." Gabriele's eyebrows shot up in surprise.

"Maybe Maria can explain it?" Lori looked at her daughter.

Maria leaned over, tracing the image with her fingertips. "I was trying to send both of you a message. That I wanted you to come. I had no idea if it would actually work." She looked up with a smile. "I guess it did."

Chapter 46

Lori sat in her office, surrounded by travel books and computer equipment. She finished putting together the travel budget to send a group to the Democratic Republic of Congo, then got up and pulled a paper cup from the dispenser on the water cooler. Lori took a long drink of cool water and turned on the radio to catch up on the news.

A reporter had just begun a breaking news story about an employee of the radio station, Amy Matthews, who had gone missing in Mendocino. She had recently turned up, saying she had been abducted at gunpoint by a group of masked men in a parking lot, then taken to a remote cabin. There, she'd discovered other people being held captive in a barn. Some she recognized from news reports. Together, they'd overcome their captors and escaped. Police Chief Moses was interviewed and said they'd searched the abandoned farm, but the abductors were long gone.

"We're just happy that after all this time, all the missing people in Nils Forest were found alive and accounted for."

It was a strange story leaving many questions unanswered. It made the rounds on cable TV news and radio talk shows, but Lori knew the police chief was too relieved to have closed all those cases to press the "victims" for any more information.

A lump formed in Lori's throat at the mention of Amy. Her memories of that terrifying night were still clear in her mind: Amy's eyes wild with fear as the white fungal threads consumed her; Maria standing there, doing nothing to help her friend. The images of the ritual haunted Lori in her quiet moments.

Lori sat back down, letting the memories pass, suppressing a wave of anxiety with deep, gulping breaths.

When her breathing returned to normal and the lump in her throat disappeared, she remembered she had some business to take care of. She'd already collected her things from the house in Mendocino. All she needed to do now was call home. Her father picked up immediately.

"How's Mom?" Lori asked.

"As well as can be expected," her father snapped. "She could use your help, you know, when you're done galivanting around Mendocino. She's far too needy for me."

"I've accepted a new job with a startup, Dad."

He gave a derisive snort.

"Is that right?" His voice dripped with condescension. "Well, maybe it's for the best. The fact is, you were always in over your head in your role. A role I gave you, you'll recall, because you couldn't find a job on your own and your mother insisted. So, I wish you luck. Let's see how long you last on your own merits."

Lori listened to her father's revisionist history and clenched her fists, her knuckles turning white. The familiar heat began to rise in her chest, and she struggled to control the surge of anger and frustration on the brink of consuming her. The fact was, her father had actually threatened to cut her off if she didn't join the business because he felt having family on the payroll was good for the company's image.

"Thank you for your kind wishes, Dad," she said, voice as hard and brittle as glass. "It's a great job, by the way. An important one, not that you care. Oh, and there's something else. I'm with Julian. You remember him? Maria's father?

We're back together now, like we should have been all these years. And you know what else? You can go to hell."

Lori ended the call and took a deep breath to steady herself. And then she laughed. Because she'd finally stood up to her bully of a father, and damn, it felt good. Still smiling, she went back to work.

When she was done for the day, Lori headed across the meadow to a small cabin. Before she could knock, Amy flung open the door.

"Finally! I thought you forgot about me."

Lori stepped past Amy into the same room Maria would have stayed in if she hadn't ventured into Nils Forest.

"Of course not." She eyed the unmade bed where Amy had spent the better part of a week after Gabriele cut her out of the mycelium cocoon.

Amy couldn't remember most of what had happened after they first met Maria at the kilns. Which was a good thing. There was less to forgive that way. She did recall having treated Maria badly and seemed truly remorseful. Amy had apologized, then surprised everyone by asking how she could help the team.

After David Eager offered to triple her old salary, Amy quit her radio job and began researching and identifying the locations where their work was needed the most. She also put together a PR campaign for when the time came to go public with their activities.

"How are you feeling today?" Lori asked.

Amy went over to a small table and poured two glasses of red wine. "Good enough to finally drink some of the good shit."

Lori accepted her glass and studied the young woman. Some color had returned to her cheeks, and the dark circles under her eyes were less pronounced.

"Have you seen Maria today?" Amy asked.

Lori shook her head. "She's either in the forest or the grow house. I hardly get to see her anymore."

Amy sniffed. "Sounds about right. She always was a bit obsessive about stuff. When she first started working at the radio station, she practically lived there. She's going to turn into a mushroom if she keeps that up."

Lori laughed. Amy had come through her experience with the fungus a nicer person, but her irreverent sense of humor remained intact.

Amy reached into the drawer of her nightstand, pulled something out, and set it on the table.

It was a small stone figurine—a gargoyle of a man with a mushroom hat. It looked old and resembled the figures painted on the ceilings of the kilns.

Lori eyed the figurine. "What's this?"

"It belongs to Maria." Amy patted it on the head. "It's a long story, but I brought it with me from the apartment, and I forgot I had it. Would you mind giving it to her for me?"

Lori sipped her wine and eyed her curiously. "Why don't you give it to her yourself?"

Amy thought for a moment. "Yeah, I probably should."

Lori set down her glass with a sigh. "Actually, I wanted to ask you a favor. I get the feeling that Maria is trying to avoid us, but I can't figure out why. Just last week, everything seemed fine. Better than fine. But she's suddenly too busy to have anything to do with me. Us. Julian too, which is strange because you know how she is about Julian." She paused long enough to point at the little figurine. "If you take that to her yourself, that gives you an excuse to see her."

"Tricky." Amy wriggled her eyebrows.

"Desperate is more like it. I'm worried.

"I've heard mothers tend to do that," Amy said with a bitter edge. "Not mine, though. She could give a rat's ass about me."

Lori reached across the table and patted her hand. "Your mom's an idiot, then. I care."

"No worries. I'll go see her and give her this thing back. It always did give me the creeps." Amy took Lori's hand and gave it a gentle squeeze. "Thank you, Lori. You've been…really cool about everything."

Lori quickly turned away so Amy wouldn't notice the tears welling up in her eyes. She'd spent days at Amy's bedside, watching over her while she recovered. And now, they had a special bond, one that stemmed from gratitude and vulnerability.

Lori could only hope that one day, she and Maria might share a similar bond.

Chapter 47

Amy found Maria in the grow house. The first thing that hit her was the humidity—cloying and thick. At least it wasn't hot. It also wasn't dark, like she'd imagined. There was plenty of natural light.

An earthy aroma filled her nose. Not exactly a bad smell, but she could do without the whiff of decay that came along with it. Amy nervously eyed a long row of mushrooms and edged away. There was no reason to fear them now. She was on their side. Maria's side. But she was still nervous. Amy found the idea of sentient mushrooms frightening and exciting at the same time. The possibilities, according to David and Gabriele, were limitless.

She spotted Maria at the far side of the room, alone, and hurried over to her.

"Hey." Amy felt awkward around her friend after all they'd been through.

Maria turned, dark eyes widening. "What are you doing here?"

"I'm not your prisoner anymore. Your goons are gone. I'm free to come and go as I please." Amy smiled to take the sting out of her words. "Am I interrupting something? Are you in the middle of whatever it is you do in here?"

Maria grimaced. "I'm sorry. About the way those guys treated you. And everything else."

Amy didn't know what to say, for once, and nodded instead. A moment later, she remembered what she had come for. She pulled the little talisman out of a pocket and set it on the counter.

Maria stared down at it, blinking.

Amy's cheeks burned. "He's been hanging out in my backpack. I wanted you to have him back, in case he's a good luck charm or something. And besides, he's yours."

"Thank you." Maria's voice was barely above a whisper.

Amy's attention shifted to the plastic containers of mushrooms. They weren't anything special to look at—their small round caps a dull red with yellowish stalks. But there was something perky about them, the way they seemed to stand at attention, bending slightly outward, as if trying to listen to their conversation.

She shivered. Mushrooms didn't have ears. At least, she didn't think so. She'd never asked Gabriele what a sentient mushroom could or couldn't do.

Amy cleared her throat. "You spend a lot of time in here," she began.

"It's where I belong. We're trying to figure out what substrates they like best." Maria seemed to notice Amy's blank look, and she quickly added, "That's the stuff the mushrooms grow in. We're testing different substrates. Straw, grain, coffee grounds. Even coconut husks."

"That sounds very sciency. I thought your job was more...mystical."

Maria laughed. "It is that too." Then the smile faded, and she looked away.

"You okay?"

Maria shrugged. "I'm just tired, that's all."

"You sure?"

Maria had always kept things close to her chest.

Another shrug. "I'm fine. Really."

Maria was lying. Amy knew her well enough to know. Lori hadn't been imagining things. Something was up. For one thing, Maria avoided looking Amy in the eye. For another, she was wearing a black sweater but was rubbing her arms as if she was cold.

The motion tugged the fabric down one shoulder, revealing a cluster of spots below her collar bone.

Amy stared. Gray lumps with irregular edges. She couldn't help it. She reached down, fingers brushing against the spots. They felt soft and slightly spongy.

Maria's eyes narrowed, and she quickly swatted Amy's hand away. "Don't."

Amy snatched her hand back. "What is *that*?"

"It's nothing." Maria angled her body away. "It's fine. Nothing to worry about."

Amy wasn't having it. "That's not nothing, Maria."

Maria lifted her chin, eyes flashing with defiance, and pulled her sweater up over her shoulder.

"Have you had that looked at? It could be pre-cancerous. My grandpa had some spots on his arm, and they zapped them off."

Maria pressed her lips together, giving a nearly imperceptible shake of her head. "It's not cancer."

A chill crawled down Amy's spine. "Maria. Seriously. You need to get that looked at. What if it's a fungal infection? They're nothing to mess around with." She paused, frown deepening. "Does Gabriele know? He must know about this stuff, maybe even how to treat it. What does he say?"

Maria was looking everywhere except at Amy. "It's not an infection, but it is fungal. Gabriele has never seen anything like it. He thinks…" Maria seemed to have a hard time getting the words out. "He thinks it's because of the new mushrooms."

Amy's eyebrows shot up "What do mean, because of the new mushrooms?"

Maria fidgeted with the hem of her sweater. "Gabriele said that the fungus is…affecting me. And that's what makes me good at what I need to do."

"Affecting you!" Amy cried. "You've got mushrooms growing out of your skin. How are you not freaking out? Is Gabriele saying you have to live with that weird shit because…you're the Spore Queen or whatever?"

Maria suddenly stood, putting a hand to her head. It was shaking slightly. "We're not sure yet. It might just be a stage. And whatever you do, do not tell Lori and Julian. There's no need to worry them."

Amy shook her head, heart racing at the surreal situation. "This is insane! You can't just ignore it and hope it goes away. And you can't keep this a secret from them. They deserve to know what's going on with you."

"The last time I checked, I was an adult." Maria's voice rose. "I have a right to a little privacy."

Amy's shoulders slumped. She had to agree with Maria on that one. As much as she'd come to like and respect Lori and Julian, what adult child told their parents everything?

"All right." Amy raked a hand through her hair. "But you're a bruja, right? Can't you use your powers to fix that shit?"

"It doesn't work like that," Maria answered briskly. "Thank you for bringing me my little mushroom guy." And then she rushed toward the door, head held high.

Chapter 48

Lori and Julian stopped in Bogota, Columbia, before taking a flight to Cucuta in the Norte de Santander District. David Eager was already there and had sent a local guide and crew to meet them at the airport, then escort them into the mountain range bordering Venezuela.

Their guide was a member of a local indigenous tribe. In an email, David had explained that Yean Agbatrai served as a land-rights defender for his people. At first, Yean had been suspicious of them, but after an excursion into the jungle with Maria, he returned determined to support their cause.

Maria had not pressed him to take the mushroom, so caution was advised. Yean was a trusted ally, but not a believer.

The crew called Lori "gringa" and seemed to be far more at ease with Julian than with this foreign white woman. They talked in Spanish, and from the laughter, there were many jokes. She found it reassuring, considering the guns they carried.

"Just in case," Julian had said. Just in case they ran into guerillas or drug traffickers still hanging around.

"They're almost all gone, señora," Yean said. "They were frightened away." Then he laughed.

One of the men stood and mimicked furious running, rocking the boat in the process.

After a long day on the river, they docked at an inlet with a small campsite. Lori and Julian were given a tiny hut. The crew would sleep in tents. When Yaen caught sight of Lori stretching and rubbing her back, he grinned and motioned for her to follow him through a thicket of trees toward a creek.

The water was a couple of feet deep and clear enough she could see the smooth, sandy bed. Steam rose from the surface.

Lori's eyes widened. "Please tell me this is a hot spring."

"Very hot," Yaen replied.

While the men busied themselves with dinner preparations, she and Julian made their way back to the water's edge. Carefully picking a path across the slickrock, they stripped off their clothes and slipped into the warm water. Lori leaned her head back and closed her eyes, the tension in her muscles melting away.

"This is amazing," she said.

When she opened her eyes, Julian was watching her. "You're amazing. I can't think of many women who would agree to come all the way out here."

Lori frowned. "I can't think of many women who have a daughter all the way out here. Doing what she's doing."

"She'll be happy to see you." Julian slipped further into the water.

Lori sighed. "Will she? I hardly saw her before she left." While her relationship with Maria had improved, her daughter still seemed more relaxed around Julian. "I'm glad you were able to spend a little time with her, though. And don't look at me like that. I'm not jealous. At least she's communicating with one of us."

"She's convinced I know more about brujeria than I'm telling her. It's a shame she never met my father. He didn't have the gift, but he knew all the old stories. I told Maria we'd take her to Mexico and see if we can track down some people she could talk to."

Lori frowned. "With everything she can do, what's there for her to learn?"

"I don't know. But she's lonely. She has no one to talk to about what's happened to her, to help her understand. I feel sorry for her."

Lori sat up straight, the weight of her worry once again pressing on her shoulders. "Are you saying she needs a mentor?"

"Of course she does," Julian replied. "And this is one area where I think I can help. I still have family back in Mexico. One of my cousins is a curandero. He should be able to point us in the right direction." He paused. "I've been thinking about this a lot, actually. She hasn't come out and asked me for an introduction, but I think it's what she needs."

Lori lowered herself back into the hot water, thinking. He was right, of course. After leaving Nils Forest, Maria had been reluctant to talk about her experiences. There wasn't anyone she could confide in who would understand.

"Mexico it is, then," she said to Julian.

After a simple dinner of arepas toasted over a smoky wood fire and topped with beans and pork rinds, Lori and Julian, relaxed by their soak in the hot spring, retreated to their hut and quickly fell asleep.

When Lori woke in the morning, she saw a semicircle of delicate purple mushrooms just outside their door.

Maria wasn't far, then. Not for the first time, Lori wondered how her daughter was able to track people's movements in the forest and send the fungi out as a greeting. Or a deterrent. She'd tried asking, but it was yet another thing Maria had refused to discuss.

Would her daughter always remain such a mystery?

After several more hours on the river, they finally reached their destination. David Eager was impatiently waiting for them in the tiny village. Lori watched him wade through the water to help pull the boat ashore, and she was once again struck by his transformation. He'd gone from an invalid hobbling on a walker to a youthful man full of energy and strength.

"You're here!" he greeted them, beaming.

Julian clapped David on the back with a grin.

"Is Maria all right?" Lori asked, stepping out of the boat and onto the muddy riverbank.

David took her arm and gave it a little squeeze. "Of course, she's all right."

"Is she here?" Lori looked around. The village was more elaborate than she had expected. A series of little huts stood in perfect formation around a small clearing. They appeared new and meticulously crafted, made of wooden walls and thatched roofs.

Instead of answering, David pointed to a large cone-shaped building at the center. "That's a long house. A communal area."

Lori was only half listening. "David, where's Maria?"

David avoided meeting her gaze and instead looked past her, toward the mountains. "She doesn't like coming to camp," he finally said.

Lori's pulse quickened, and she pictured Maria in the jungle, alone. This wasn't Nils Forest. This was a foreign country, the Norte Santander District, filled with cocaine farms and armed men determined to defend them. When she first learned Maria had chosen this place to begin their mission, Lori had loudly objected, but her protests fell on deaf ears.

"She's out there alone?" Lori pressed, voice rising.

Julian hurried over and slung a reassuring arm around her shoulders. "She's not alone. Gabriele's with her. Yaen said some of his best men are with them too."

"But when can we see her?" she demanded.

"Soon enough." David then walked toward their hut.

His cryptic reply made her want to shake him. Lori wouldn't be happy until she'd seen Maria with her own eyes. She wanted to see Maria was all right, that she was happy.

Chapter 49

Lori hardly tasted her dinner that night.

Falling asleep was nearly impossible. The forest was noisy with animals, and as she tossed and turned in her cot, the wind began to pick up, whistling and howling through the leaves of their thatched roof and the canopy of trees. Beside her, Julian began to stir.

A clap of thunder made them both jump. Flashes of light could be seen in the gap around the door. Lori shivered, recalling those terrible ceremonies in Nils Forest, and followed Julian outside. David was already there, a blanket over his shoulders. Yaen stood beside him.

The air was thick with humidity, but there was no rain. Lightning flashed, lighting the ridge of trees and illuminating a mass of storm clouds. Lori forced herself not to blink and silently began to count the lightning flashes. Fifteen, twenty, then thirty. In what, less than a minute? The sound was unlike anything she had ever heard, resonating deep within her bones.

"What's happening?" she shouted over the din of the crackling thunder.

David turned toward her, eyes as wild as his unruly hair. "I told you not to worry," he said triumphantly.

Julian's arm encircled her waist and pulled her closer.

"Is this Maria?" Lori asked.

David leaned toward her. "Not her alone." He gave a meaningful nod at Yaen, who still stared at the light show in the sky.

"Has this ever happened before?" Julian asked.

David grinned. "No." He pulled them away from Yaen and the others before continuing. "This is the thirtieth night running. It's just the lightning now, but it started with a pyramid and a summoning and a few ceremonies. Enough to spread the message that a new boss was in town. And the coca growers couldn't get out fast enough. And there's more progress too. I'll show you in the morning."

The gusts and lightning continued through the night, only stopping in the small hours before dawn. Lori dreamed of ancient realms and of the wind whispering secrets.

She woke with a pounding headache.

David and his endless supply of money had ensured the camp was well outfitted, so after a couple of ibuprofen and several steaming mugs of coffee, Lori dressed and followed Julian and David into the forest.

They didn't need to go far to see what David wanted to show them. White fungal mats covered the forest floor, glowing faintly in the dim morning light.

"It's working." David smiled proudly. "Gabriele and his team introduced the new fungi into areas around the coca farms. It killed the plants in a matter of days, and the soil is already beginning to recover—"

"So fast?" Julian interrupted.

"So fast. The team has already moved on to areas deforested by mining and cattle, and they're seeing progress there too. Of course." His expression turned solemn. "Everything is moving fast, even our medical startup. This is unconventional, to say the least, but we've started some experimental trials—"

It was Lori's turn to interrupt. "On people? Doesn't the FDA need to be involved?"

David's eyes twinkled, and he held a finger to his lips. "Let's just say it's off the books. The people who are taking part have given their full consent, and a few might even be on the board."

They ventured further into the forest. Mushrooms began to appear and multiply, sprouting in impossible shapes and sizes, some towering as large as small trees. David guided them to a mushroom grove. Julian was shaking his head in wonder, but Lori was too tense to enjoy the otherworldly surroundings.

"Isn't anybody noticing this? And don't they think it's a problem?" Julian asked.

David chuckled. "That's the beauty of this location. It's too remote for most people, and the locals aren't about to complain. They just want peace and to get their land back."

Lori's thoughts kept returning to Maria. Where was she in this vast forest? Her headache returned, more painful than before. She was about to ask if they could turn back when she bumped into an enormous white mushroom growing out of a tree. It exploded, releasing a cloud of microscopic particles dancing in the air. She batted at them, sputtering.

Alarmed, Julian pulled Lori away and sat her down on a rock. Several anxious moments passed, but nothing happened. Nothing except for a calm washing over her, accompanied by a strange sense of clarity. Or maybe it was anticipation.

"Are you all right?" Julian asked, cautiously releasing his grip on her arm.

Lori took a deep breath, feeling the clean air fill her lungs. "I'm fine," she murmured.

And she was. Her headache was gone.

Chapter 50

Their second night in the mountain camp, the lightning show returned. Despite the flashing lights and the constant racket of thunder, Julian slept soundly. Restless, Lori slipped outside, a blanket over her shoulders. She was alone, except for something rustling in the trees at the edge of the clearing.

Pulse quickening, Lori nervously scanned the canopy. She shivered, hoping it was a monkey or a coati. Yaen or David hadn't said anything about jaguars, but they had them in Columbia, didn't they?

She hurried into the hut and grabbed a flashlight. When its beam illuminated the trees, she gasped.

Maria was suspended among the branches, her long hair cascading down her back. Lori's heart felt like it had detonated in her chest. Her ears rang, and her pulse raced, a shock surging through her body.

She could no longer deny her daughter was a bruja.

The very laws of nature had bent to Maria's will.

Lori couldn't bear to look any longer. Tears welling in her eyes, a cry escaping her throat, she turned her head.

And then Maria was standing in front of her. Despite the heat, she wore a scarf wound around her neck, and long sleeves covered her arms. Julian had come out of the hut holding a lantern, his eyes wide, staring at their daughter. The light cast an eerie glow over Maria's face. She had grown pale. There were dark circles under her eyes.

"Maria." Julian's hand found Lori's, offering silent support.

Lori struggled to find her voice, the questions choking her throat dry.

Maria gazed back at them, chin lifting, eyes glittering with excitement. "I'm glad you came. It's working. It's actually working. Has David shown you around? When we first got here, none of this vegetation was here. It was bare and ugly. But the fungus is transforming the land, like…"

"Like magic," Julian said, his voice hoarse, barely above a whisper.

"A very powerful magic," Maria agreed. "The new fungus is doing even more than I'd hoped. It's helping the native plants grow back faster. Gabriele says the air and soil quality have improved too."

While Maria went on about the new fungus, Lori's thoughts returned to what David had said earlier that day in the forest.

She studied her daughter in the glow of the electric lantern. Maria'd lost weight. Her cheekbones were more pronounced, and her complexion was pale and waxy, nearly transparent. Perhaps it was just a trick of the light, but Maria's appearance gave Lori a sense of foreboding.

She was Maria's mother, and a mother's instinct told her something was wrong.

Lori held up a hand. "Maria," she interrupted. "Is everything okay? Are *you* okay?"

Maria's eyes flicked upward. They'd missed the teenage years together, but that's what Maria resembled now—a teenage girl annoyed with mom's interruption.

"I'm fine," Maria said curtly. "It's just a part of the process. You wouldn't understand."

Lori's protective instincts flared at that cryptic remark. She stepped back for a better look at her daughter.

Julian wasn't having it. He placed both hands on Maria's shoulders and turned her toward him. To Lori's surprise, Maria didn't resist. Her lower lip began to tremble.

When he spoke, it was with a father's voice. Concerned. Demanding. "What's that supposed to mean? What's going on, mija?"

"It's nothing," she whispered. But she couldn't meet his eyes. She was looking at Lori now, pleading.

"Whatever it is, you can tell us, honey," Lori said. Her voice was calm, while her insides screamed.

"I can't do this," Maria cried. She turned and ran toward the dark cover of the forest, feet lifting off the ground at the edge of the clearing.

Lori covered her mouth with her hands and watched Maria rise into the air. As she flew over the treetops, Maria gave an anguished cry of heartbreak.

Chapter 51

David joined them for their final night in Bogota before heading back to the states. Afterward, they sat in the hotel bar, drinking red wine.

In the face of their many questions about Maria, David looked grave and resolute. "Nothing's wrong. Maria knows how important this work is, and she's feeling the stress."

Lori stared at him. "No. It's more than stress. I can sense it." She turned toward Julian. "You can feel it too, right?"

She knew he did because they'd talked of nothing else since last seeing Maria in the jungle of Norte de Sander. Their daughter had never returned to the camp, and no one would tell them where she was headed next.

Julian nodded.

"I understand you're worried." David lowered his voice. "Here's what I can tell you. She's in closer communication with the fungi. The messages are becoming more specific, more detailed, and constant. She can't shut them out, and it's all a bit overwhelming. Gabriele believes it's all part of the process, and eventually, they'll arrive at a mutually acceptable symbiosis."

A heavy silence settled over them. Lori placed her glass of wine on the table and gripped the arms of her chair as if it were about to take off. "What if it kills her?" she asked at last.

David topped off his glass. "It won't. It needs her."

Julian squeezed her hand. "And she's a powerful bruja, don't forget."

"How could I ever?" The memory of her daughter flying off into the night sky was forever burned into her brain.

"You worry too much."

Lori drained the last of her wine. Julian might trust him, but she didn't. David Eager was lying. She was sure of it.

Before Julian was awake, Lori went downstairs and called Amy from a quiet spot in the lobby. Without preamble, she demanded to know where Maria was headed next.

"I'm not supposed to say," Amy said.

"I need to see my daughter. Something's not right."

Amy cleared her throat. "I think so too." A long silence followed before she continued. "Okay. I'll tell you. I owe you that. And I'm worried too, if you want to know the truth. They're going to the Congo Basin Forest in the Democratic Republic of Congo. They'll be focusing on some areas deforested by commercial logging. David thought it was too dangerous to go into another place with a lot of armed conflict, so the DRC seemed safest. They'll expand from there."

Amy paused, as though a new thought had just occurred to her.

"If you hurry, I think you can beat them to the airport in Kinshasa." She hesitated. "I heard they ran into a little hiccup back at camp, so they're getting a late start."

Lori's heart fluttered. "What kind of hiccup?"

"I don't know exactly. You know how David is. He can be pretty tight-lipped when he wants to be, but they're stopping at a clinic Gabriele knows about in Italy."

Lori's mouth went dry. She could hardly get the words out. "Oh my god. Is Maria sick?"

"Maybe."

Amy sounded uncharacteristically tentative. Which meant she, too, knew more than she was telling. Pressing her would be a waste of time. Besides, Lori already had the information she wanted. She would see Maria for herself.

When they hung up, Amy texted the flight details to Lori. The concierge helped Lori book their flights to Kinshasa, leaving that evening.

After breakfast, Lori and Julian quickly packed their bags and took a cab to the airport, nervous something might happen to prevent them from making the plane. A delay would mean missing Maria in Kinshasa. During the flights, they barely spoke, Lori too lost in her own thoughts about Maria to keep up a conversation. Eventually, she fell into a fitful sleep, and when she woke, they were touching down.

They stepped off the aircraft and were met by a blast of humid heat. Lori and Julian found a hotel and, the next day, returned to the airport. They approached the terminal, the hot sun bearing down on them, when a plane landed.

People streamed through security and headed toward the baggage claim area. Finally, Gabriele emerged. Beside him was a slight figure wearing a strange ensemble. A hat covered in a veil. Long sleeves. Pants. Socked feet in sandals. It had to be Maria.

Julian stiffened beside her. "What the hell?" He clutched Lori's arm.

When Gabriele spotted Julian, he froze. But there was no way to avoid them. Shoulders slumping, he trudged toward them, his hand gripping his companion's elbow.

Heads bent together, Maria and Gabriele stopped a few feet away.

"Mija," Julian said. The worry in his voice nearly broke Lori's heart.

"Dad." It was Maria. Of course, it was Maria. That same voice, thick with emotion.

Her daughter was behind the veil, hiding. Hiding from them and the world. And Gabriele had known all about it. By the look of shame on his face, it was bad, and he'd hidden it from them, either of his own accord or because Maria had demanded it.

"Lori," Gabriele said.

"Don't," she snapped. "We're not here to see you."

Gabriele turned away, red-faced.

"It's okay," Maria said from behind the ridiculous veil.

Except for a few workers bustling around the security screening area, they were alone. With a gloved hand, Maria slowly lifted the veil. Julian's body gave an involuntary jerk against Lori.

Maria's face was covered in a web of fine white strands. On one cheek, poking out between the filaments, a tiny pale mushroom sprouted.

Lori gasped.

Julian's grip tightened on Lori's arm, and he swayed on his feet. "Oh no, Maria."

Gabriele shifted. He was staring at them now, eyes glistening. "It might be okay. She's on a new medication. She seems a little better. Right, Maria?"

Lori backed away from her daughter. Her beautiful, brilliant daughter. The child she'd given away and driven to this.

If she'd kept her baby, raised her with Julian and the heritage that was rightly hers, Maria wouldn't have had that empty hole that needed to be filled by someone—something—out to exploit her. Lori continued backing up until she was pressed against a wall of glass and could go no farther.

This time, Maria stared past her father and at Lori, eyes pleading. And then Maria was walking toward her, the veil back in place.

"Thank you for coming," Maria whispered, sounding on the verge of tears. "This might be a gift and not a curse. Eventually, I'll find out which it is." She paused. "Are you going to leave?"

Lori reached around and rubbed Maria's back for a moment. Beneath the fabric of her daughter's loose shirt, spongy knobs met her fingers. She snatched her hand away. The veil twitched, and Maria gave a little sob.

Tears blurred Lori's vision, but with a smile on her lips, she said, "Never again."

Trembling, she reached out and touched her daughter's gloved hand. A white filament slithered out from beneath the cuff and wrapped itself around Lori's wrist. Together, connected, mother and daughter made their way through the terminal.

The End

Debra Castaneda

Author's Note

If you've visited the charming town of Mendocino and wonder how the heck you missed Nils Forest, you didn't—it was invented for this story.

For that matter, the behavior of the fungus in this story is exaggerated too. I took some supernatural liberties after studying the amazing world of mushrooms. I always enjoy researching my books, but this was a particularly fascinating journey. If you're curious about the incredible secret life of fungus, I highly recommend two excellent books: Entangled Life by Merlin Sheldrake and Paul Stamet's Mycelium Running.

The Spore Queen was originally going to be the first book in the Dark Earth Rising series. The subject of out-of-control fungus was suggested to me by a friend and scientist, Carolyn. She told me about a tree-killing honey fungus that is the largest single organism in the world, located in Oregon.

Many a rabbit hole did I fall into after hearing that story. The problem was, I needed a hook for The Spore Queen, and that was more challenging than I expected. It took me quite a while and several other Dark Earth Rising novels, but I finally found it. I'm not sure I would have attempted fungal horror without Carolyn's encouragement. She's also very fun to hang out with. That's why this novel is dedicated to her.

Two more bits of a personal nature. If you've read The Devil's Shallows, you may remember the minor character who suffered from Lewy Body dementia, the same disease that afflicted my father. I thought I was done writing about it until this story began to take shape. The hallucinations that troubled my dad had struck me as particularly cruel and horrific. Simply put, there was more for me to work through, so I enlisted the help of retired tech mogul David Eager in this book.

The other personal issue that surfaced in this book is adoption. I like to joke that I'm "double Mexican." Both my birth mother and adoptive parents were of Mexican descent. Growing up, I used to fantasize about my birth parents, probably because I was denied information about them. It was only after I was well into writing the first draft of The Spore Queen that I realized I had unintentionally given voice to my adolescent fantasy of my birth parents coming to look for me. Adoption is a very specific experience for adoptees and birth mothers, and this story is not meant as a broader statement about either.

Finally, a shoutout to my amazing editor, friend and supporter, Lyndsey Smith of Horrorsmith Editing, and to Tiffany Koplin, R.J. Roles and the other admins of the Books of Horror Facebook group for creating such a supportive space for indie authors..

.

Keep Reading for a Preview of

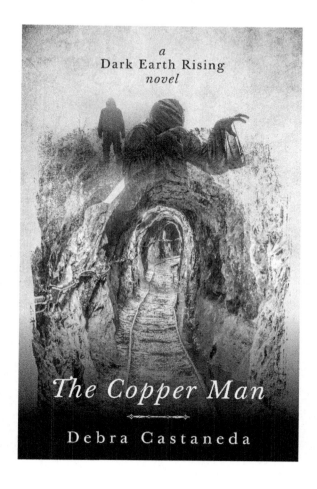

a
Dark Earth Rising
novel

The Copper Man

Debra Castaneda

Some grudges never die.

Chapter 1

George Cunliffe teetered on the edge of the Lower Prestwich Bridge, his back to the yawning open-pit mine and everything that had made his life a misery.

What he did not feel was guilt. What he had done, he would do again.

He could not remember the drive to the mine, where he had left his truck with the evidence inside, or how he'd come to choose this spot to end his life.

Oblivious to the icy wind against his face, he stared down at the enormous tailings pond, the liquid a reddish orange on one side, running to a sickly yellowish green on the other.

The wind pushed the hood of his jacket from his head. Wooden floor beams of the old trestle bridge groaned beneath his feet.

Time to get going.

His hands were stiff but steady as he tested the strength of the vertical post closest to him and found it solid. After looping the old, frayed rope around the base of the iron shaft, he tied a knot, then slipped the noose around his neck. He'd intended to get right to it—leap into the air, arms spread wide, welcoming death—but he found he wanted to prolong his time on the bridge, just a little. Long enough to remember the one good, beautiful thing in his pathetic life that had brought him joy.

He picked up a small rock from the railbed and scratched words into the rusted track. When he was done, he tossed the rock into the tailings pond and admired his work.

I CURSE THIS PLACE.

Lowering himself onto the rail ties, he swung his legs over the side, one hand gripping a diagonal brace. He kicked off his boots and flicked the rope behind his neck, as if it were a scarf getting in his way. Then, before he could think about another thing, he pushed himself off.

A scream escaped his lips.

He hadn't meant to scream. The noise ended abruptly, and for one long moment, pain seared his neck as the rope tightened. His hands flew up to the noose, fingers clawing at the fibers, and then he was falling.

His body slammed into the pond's sludgy, sucking bank.

He lay there for how long?

Seconds? Minutes?

The rope had snapped, that much he understood. Even though death was not instantaneous, it was surely just a matter of minutes. His insides had to be smashed to bits. His mouth tasted like blood and metal. He stared up at the sky, the clouds turning a murky and sinister orange.

Or was the copper color of the water altering his vision?

Rain drops hit his face, sharp and distinct. By some miracle, he was still alive, standing. Floating above the tailings pond. He gazed down at his still body in wonder.

Transformed. That's what he was. His thoughts came in flashes. Images. Thinking in this strange new language.

His old life was over. His mind—the one that had been attached to his broken body—had carried over into this new, strange existence he'd yet to explore. It was like a warm yellow glow coming from under a door. He yearned to push it open and see what was there. Or *who* was there.

"Son?" he cried.

Instead, he heard the distant shouting of men and felt the wetness of rain falling upon his face. Then all was dark, except his mind.

More Books by Debra Castaneda

Dark Earth Rising
Themed novels that can be read in any order

A Dark and Rising Tide
When a massive storm surge hits the central coast of California, the ferocious surf destroys buildings, floods streets, and washes up something sinister from the depths of the Monterey Bay.

The Devil's Shallows
Eight miles of mystery. One night of terror. Residents trapped in a remote neighborhood confront the unimaginable.

The Copper Man
Haunted tunnels. Unexplained deaths. Eerie sightings. Decades after The Copper Man killed her brother, Leah Shaw returns to the remote mining town of Tribulation Gulch where a lethal mystery awaits.

The Root Witch
A beautiful forest. A terrifying legend. It's 1986. Two strangers, hundreds of miles apart, grapple with disturbing incidents in a one-of-a-kind quaking aspen forest.

Circus at Devil's Landing
Creatures that howl in the night, a mysterious circus, and a clash between a ringmaster and a woman determined to rescue her captured lover.

Chavez Ravine Novels
Stand-alone novels set in Chavez Ravine, Los Angeles during turbulent times

The Monsters of Chavez Ravine
A 2021 International Latino Book Awards Gold Medal Winner! Before Dodger Stadium, dark forces terrorized Chavez Ravine.

The Night Lady
A rebel curandera, a plucky seamstress, and a young reporter are pulled into the investigation of a killer terrorizing Chavez Ravine.